BLOOD MOON
HEAT

BLOOD MOON BRIDES, BOOK TWO

SHERILEE GRAY

Epub ISBN: 978-1-0670019-7-1

Print ISBN: 978-1-0670019-8-8

Content Note: Dubious consent, consensual non-consent, blood play, fear play, primal play

Prologue

〜

MINA

Two years ago

I LAY STILL as my bedroom window silently lifted.

It was him.

He was back.

The first time he came was the night of my sixteenth birthday. He'd stood outside, watching me through the pink lace curtains. I'd been afraid, unable to move, clutching the covers to myself as if that could protect me. He'd stayed out there for several hours, soundless, unmoving, then finally left.

The next day the vampire court informed my parents that my mate had come to them, that he was powerful, one of The Five, and he'd notified them of his intention to claim me when I came of age.

It was a full year before I saw him again. Once again, he'd stood at my window, so impossibly still, his deep violet eyes glowing through the shadows. He'd remained there, watching me for so long, I hadn't been able to keep my eyes open, and somehow, I'd drifted off with that cold, hard gaze burning into me.

I probably should have been scared then, and I should be now, as he opened the window wide and stepped into my room another year later. I'd been expecting him, it was the night of my eighteenth birthday, but he'd never come into my room before.

My heart thudded wildly in my chest. My father always said I was too curious for my own good, that fear was healthy, that it stopped us from doing idiotic things that would get us killed. But I hadn't been made that way. I mean, obviously, I felt fear, and the first time my mate came to the window, I'd definitely felt it. But fear had always...excited me, exhilarated me. And it wasn't like he'd ever actually done anything besides watch me.

Was he going to talk to me this time? I inwardly cringed. My bedroom looked like someone had projectile vomited lace and silk all over it, but worse, all of it was in eye-watering shades of pink. Princess-chic my mother had called it. I hated it, and I hated pink—or at least I did now—but that didn't matter to her. It was as if she thought a pink, lacy horror show of a bedroom would make me the female she wished I was. I only hoped the male soundlessly moving across the room didn't think it was a reflection of my personality. I was no delicate little princess.

He stopped at the foot of my bed, and I kept my eyes screwed shut, gripping my covers to my chest, but the way my heart raced, he had to know I was awake. Still, I wasn't afraid, not really. This was my mate. He wouldn't hurt me.

My skin prickled and a wave of heat washed over me out of nowhere. I flushed hot, sweat immediately prickling my skin. I wanted to shove the covers off, but I couldn't; he was just there, and it wouldn't be proper for me to lie here in only my nightgown.

My mouth was suddenly bone dry. There was a glass of water on my bedside table, but I didn't dare reach for it. I kept up my pretense of sleep, waiting for what would come next.

I listened for the sound of him breathing, but he wasn't. I listened harder. His heart wasn't beating, either, which meant he was very old, or he'd been so badly injured at some point that his heart had stopped. Maybe both. I barely contained a shiver at the thought.

As the hours ticked by—he stood motionless, utterly silent while I feigned sleep—my overheated skin grew hotter and tingly, and my shallow breaths turned to pants.

There was an ache between my thighs that had been slowly increasing as well and now it throbbed. I tried so hard not to move, but if I didn't squeeze my thighs together to relieve the terrible ache, I'd cry. I couldn't bear it another moment and gave in, squeezing my thighs together tight. A whimper escaped. It was small, but as soon as it left my mouth, a growl long and deep rolled over me from the foot of the bed.

Oh gods.

Finally, gathering my courage, I opened my eyes—but he was gone.

One year later

I was dying.

My body was burning up, and the deep, throbbing pain between my thighs had me squirming in my sheets. I lifted my head, refusing to pretend I didn't know he was there, not this time.

My mate stood at the foot of my bed, his face concealed in shadow. He said nothing. He didn't move. Not an inch. He just watched as I writhed and panted and sobbed in pain.

God, I wanted to beckon him to me, I wanted him to...gods, to touch me, to help me. He'd done this. Somehow, he was doing this to me. Last time, I'd suffered for days after he left. Sweating and crying, the pain in my lower belly and between my thighs so acute I thought I'd die. In my mind, I'd screamed for him. I'd screamed and screamed, but he never came. My parents didn't know what was wrong with me, and I'd been too afraid to tell them the truth.

His head tilted to the side, studying me coldly, like I was some kind of fascinating insect, or an experiment.

Why was he doing this to me?

I shoved the covers off, too hot to stay beneath them a moment longer. My skin was on fire, my hair plastered to the sides of my face. My nightgown, damp with sweat, clung to my body, and when I squeezed my legs together, they were slick. Embarrassment filled me, and heat rushed to my cheeks.

I stared into the shadows, into those glowing violet eyes. "Help me," I begged, knowing instinctively that only he could take this pain away. "It hurts. Please...help me."

Every year he came to my room, I felt the connection between us grow stronger. How could he ignore it? How could he let me suffer this way? I shoved my hand between my thighs, pressing my palm to my swollen, slick flesh, desperately trying to ease the emptiness, the agony. I squeezed my eyes closed as another wave of humiliation washed through me. "Please," I said again.

Just like last time, when I opened my eyes, he was gone.

One year and two days later

I was drifting off when the sound of my window opening reached me.

My twentieth birthday had been two days ago. I assumed he'd taken pity on me, that he'd decided not to come. I'd been wrong. Relief and terror filled me at the same time, and I hated the part of me that wanted this, that had anticipated his visit. What was wrong with me that the moment he left my room a year ago, I'd wanted him to come back, that I'd craved the presence of this twisted monster even when he caused me pain, when it had taken days to finally subside.

Just being near him turned me into someone else.

I gritted my teeth. *No.* I didn't want to feel this way. This wasn't right.

I scrambled out of bed and ran for the door. Not this time. I wouldn't let him do this to me again.

One moment he was by the window. The next he was at the door, blocking my escape.

He stood only inches from me, the closest I'd ever been to him. He was tall, towering over me, his shoulders broad and his muscles straining his jacket. I took in the rest of him. The skin on the side of his throat, the side that wasn't tattooed, was impossibly pale, and the shadows seemed to move with him, concealing his face from me still, all except for his eyes. They glowed bright, boring into me.

The scent of blood hit me. *His.* I knew this because my fangs tingled and my stomach growled. And someone else's blood as well —not vampire but something *other*. I scanned his body. He wore a suit, and the knuckles of his tattooed hands were grazed and red. The fact that his injuries were unhealed meant he'd done it very recently—or the wounds had been really bad. He had to have come to me immediately after he'd done whatever it was that caused those wounds.

He'd been at the border, fighting the fae—that had to be it. Was that why he'd been late coming to me?

I stumbled back, not from my fear of him—although I was old enough now to know I should be—but from my fear of what he did to me when he came here. Of how the scent of his blood called out to me and the pain and anguish I suffered for days after he left. The grip in my gut, the connection I felt for him, was stronger than it'd ever been, though I felt nothing but cold indifference rolling off him in return.

My stomach churned. I was just a curiosity to him, nothing more.

Still, my body ignited, fire burning in my belly and the pulse between my thighs beating so strongly, it forced the breath from my lungs. My skin was instantly coated in a cold sweat even as my body went up in flames. My nipples tightened painfully, and I crossed my arms to hide them. Humiliation had me looking at my feet, and as soon as I looked away from him, I was able to think more clearly, and the humiliation quickly turned to anger.

After his last visit, I'd been determined to find out why I reacted this way around him. When my parents had been out, I'd sneaked into the library and taken a book on vampire physiology that I'd been forbidden to read.

I'd learned the truth.

If a vampire was powerful and old, like the male standing in front of me, they could sense their mates early, and because of that, they were supposed to stay away until their female's twenty-first birthday, to protect her from a "need her body wasn't ready for" the book had said.

During the blood moon ceremony, when a bride was claimed, the male and his bride would drink from each other. The act was called being "blood bonded," and had to be done under the blood moon. Once it was done, the pain I felt when he was near would stop for me. The males, however, would feel something like I was now if they didn't mate right after the exchange of blood. The books said "they would feel increased hunger and a desperate need for release that would turn to intense pain if left unsatisfied." I wasn't sure what mating entailed, and a release of what, I didn't know, but if it felt anything like the pain I'd experienced, it would be unbearable. It also said "if a male was forced beyond that point, he could revert to a primal state and experience loss of control." I didn't know what that meant, either, but it didn't sound good.

I grabbed for the wall when the ache throbbed harder. "Are you going to just stand there, watching me until I'm writhing in agony, then leave me suffering for days like you always do?" I said through gritted teeth. "Or are you going to help me?"

Please, help me. God, I hated that I needed him so badly.

He said nothing, just watched me. Always watching. Screw

him. I turned my back and strode across the room. I couldn't escape him, but I refused to stand that close to him.

"What kind of help do you think you need, Mina?"

His deep, icy voice rolled through the room, stopping me in my tracks. It was the first time I'd heard it, and a shiver slid through me as I spun back. "I—I don't know. I just... I need the pain to stop." The physiology book hadn't gone into detail. But I did know it had to do with mating, that only my mate could stop this pain.

He took a step closer. "You're not ready for me to take the pain away, female."

I could only assume he was right about that, but anything had to be better than this. "Then why are you here? Why are you doing this to me?"

Another pause. "Because you fascinate me."

"And your curiosity is more important than the pain that coming here causes me?"

I hadn't expected my mate to be some white knight from one of the fairy-tale books I'd read as a child. But I hadn't expected him to be cruel.

"You don't like it, the pain?"

Dread coiled inside me. "Of course not," I whispered, not only scared of the way he made me feel, but now my fear of *him* grew even more intense.

"Explain it to me," he said, his voice growing deeper. "Tell me how it feels."

My body ached and throbbed, craving something, something from him that I didn't truly understand, while he stood there, seemingly enjoying my agony. The horror of that made me want to shrivel in on myself. I straightened and forced myself to look into his cold, dead eyes. I wanted him to see the fear that I knew was in mine, and I wanted him to watch as it drained away and changed to anger. I let the pain coursing through my body, the pain he was causing, fuel the fire. Then I smiled, and it wasn't a nice one. "I don't need to explain it. You'll find out for yourself. I promise you that."

Then I turned away from him again, giving him my back as I stared out the window.

Silence filled the room, so acute it was deafening. I thought he'd silently left, like he always did, but then something cool brushed my shoulder. His cold fingers slid across my skin, lifting goose bumps all over me. His chest brushed my back, and I gasped. But I refused to run. I stood my ground as he brushed my hair aside and leaned closer.

A rumble vibrated from his chest and moved right through me. "I look forward to it, Mina."

Then he was gone.

One

MINA

I PLACED my trembling hands against my stomach as my mother did up the choker that had been waiting here for me on our arrival. It was white gold and studded with pink diamonds.

"This must have been very expensive," my mother said a little breathlessly. "Your mate is generous, Mina, that's a very good sign."

The jewelry was nice enough, but the male who gifted it to me was most definitely not, and as my mother fastened the heavy chain, it felt like hands being wrapped around my throat—like a claiming of some kind.

"There. It looks beautiful," she said, beaming at my reflection in the mirror.

I forced a smile in return, but only because I could see how nervous she was. Unlike me, she didn't know who was coming to take me away tonight. The identity of our mates had been kept a secret even from our parents. It was safer that way.

All she knew was he was one of The Five, warriors all and the most ruthless, terrifying, and brutal vampires of our race, males who had spent their lives patrolling the borders of our territory, and protecting our kind. Our people spoke about them in reverent, hushed tones, as if they were a myth or a legend.

The Five needed to be able to travel in and out of our enemies' territories undetected, so their identities were a closely guarded secret. They were powerful males who moved in and out of society, never revealing who they were, and therefore never getting the recognition they deserved for all they'd done for us.

Tonight, the veil would be lifted.

A new fae king had been crowned, the war had ended, and The Five were rejoining society for good and would be lauded as heroes.

No, I didn't know the name of the male who came to me every year, taking pleasure in tormenting me, in watching me suffer, ignoring the rules that had been created to protect me from pain and humiliation, but I did know a male like that was most definitely not a hero.

He was a twisted psychopath.

"Everything has been arranged, and your bags have been taken to the parking garage and will be collected by your mate's driver," Mother said.

I nodded.

Worry filled her eyes. "Are you nervous? I have an elixir I purchased. It's very good for steadying nerves."

"I'm a little nervous, but I'll be okay," I said, downplaying what I was feeling for her benefit. Besides, those elixirs Mother bought from a store in Seventh Circle were potent, and I needed my wits about me tonight.

"You can take comfort knowing that you're not alone in the way you're feeling."

Four other females were somewhere here in the Grande Rozala. The ancient castle on the outskirts of Roxburgh was reserved for special occasions and ceremonies, and it was far enough from the city that it felt like another time and place. But what was happening here tonight was also happening elsewhere. Blood moon ceremonies were about to take place all over the city.

Others would be preparing for their mates to claim them, but unlike me and the other four females here tonight, their males would have sensed them at an appropriate age. They would have introduced themselves to their female and her family. The couple would have dated for a while, allowing their bond to grow at a natural rate.

They would have fallen in love, like most beings did.

"Now, Mina..." Mother cleared her throat. "There are some things I need to prepare you for...things that will happen tonight." She dipped her gaze, no longer meeting my eyes. "First, your mate will drink from you, and you from him. This must happen before the blood moon goes down, bonding you together."

I nodded, even though I knew this from the book I'd sneaked from our library.

Unlike some much older vampires, my parents weren't emotionless. They were in love. Something I'd desperately wanted for myself but knew now would never happen for me.

Mother's cheeks were flushed when she looked back up at me. "I know you've never fed from the vein before, but you must not be afraid. You are a vampire. It's how it's supposed to be. It is..." She cleared her throat. "It's natural, and very enjoyable. But your mate will guide you. He'll explain how it should be done."

"Then what happens after that, after the feeding?" I asked. I knew there was more to becoming mates, I just had no idea what that *more* was. I'd already been cosseted, like a lot of female vampires were. My knowledge had been restricted, but the last four years it had been so much worse. No friends, no outside influences that could corrupt me. I had to be innocent in all ways for my powerful mate.

She chewed her lip, a strange expression on her face as she dragged the brush through my blond hair. "You will be bound together...but there is one more step, to um...make you mates in truth."

I turned to her. "What step?"

"Males and females are made...very differently. We are designed to...to fit together."

I frowned. "Together?"

"Oh dear," she whispered, looking flustered.

"Mother? What am I supposed to do?"

She wrung her hands. "You will lie on his bed...without, uh... underwear."

I froze, heat washing through me with force. We were forbidden to touch ourselves there, not in a way that didn't involve the use of the bathroom or personal hygiene. I had, however, explored that part of myself more than I should have. How could I not when it had ached so badly, making me squirm and slick. Something had happened when that male had visited me, something dark and terrifying, something that created a longing inside me that I didn't know how to fulfill.

"Your mate will lie on top—"

There was a knock at the door.

"Come in," Mother called quickly, visibly sagging.

"On top of what—"

My father walked in, cutting me off, his lips curling in a gentle smile. "You look lovely, Mina."

"Thank you, Father." I wanted my mother to finish what she was going to say. I wanted to know what was going to happen.

He held out his hands. "It's time."

Oh gods.

"You'll be fine," Mother said, holding my gaze. "Everything will be fine."

I curled my hand around my father's arm, and we made our way out of the room and down the staircase.

Four other females and their fathers joined us at the bottom, and the nervous energy was so thick around us, I was having trouble catching my breath.

Lining up in front of a set of grand double doors, we stood there like lambs going to slaughter. One of the girls took an abrupt step back before quickly composing herself when her father muttered something in her ear.

Then two young males stepped forward, and I held my breath as they pushed the double doors wide.

All chatter from beyond the doors stopped, the room went silent, and all eyes turned our way.

One of the males stepped forward and, first clearing his throat, began to introduce us to the gathered crowd, telling them who our families were, reintroducing us to society since we'd been ensconced in our homes, hidden away, for the last five years.

"Miss Mina Angelos. Daughter of Nicholas and Serra Angelos." My name was the fourth called, and I straightened my spine, stepping forward with my father, and hoped no one saw how badly I was shaking.

My parents inclined their heads, and electricity seemed to crack through the room as anticipation grew. As much as I wanted to look around to see who was there, I did as I was told and kept my gaze trained ahead. The last female's name was announced, and she lined up beside me.

"Now, please welcome our honored guests. Warriors all, and protectors of our race," the male by the door announced. "Stefan Valiente, Rainer Beiste, August Drapała, Nero Kossek..."

The crowd of vampires stepped back quickly as, one by one, the warriors strode into the room.

Four males walked in. My monster walking in last. His gaze was deep violet, blazing as it locked on me. He was a predator. I already knew that. But he wasn't even trying to pretend to be civilized on this sacred night.

Nero Kossek. I finally knew his name.

The massive vampires stood opposite us. They were the only ones who were supposed to know which of us would be their bride. But unlike the females beside me, I knew. I knew exactly who would be taking me home with him tonight.

Confusion rumbled through the room, and I realized we were still missing one warrior.

One of the males broke away from the group, and I watched as he walked up to his bride, taking her by the hand and leading her away from the lineup. Anticipation throbbed through me so hard I felt dizzy.

The next two warriors came forward, claiming their females. Then it was my turn.

Nero closed in, his measured steps eating up the space between us. I wanted to step back, to run, but I held my ground and lifted my chin.

"Mina," he said softly for my ears only, the velvet of his voice lifting goose bumps all over me. "We meet again, finally."

It had been a full year. He hadn't come on my twenty-first birthday, apparently, he could wait the week between then and now to torment me. I stood stiffly, looking up at him, and when he reached for my hand, I jerked it back before I knew I was going to do it.

His expression didn't change. It remained frozen, like I suspected his heart was. Then slowly, unnaturally, he lifted his hand and placed it on my shoulder. I tried not to, but I jolted from the contact, my breath sticking in my throat as he slid it down my arm and wrapped his cold hand around mine.

My breath shuddered as he led me to the side with the others.

That's when I realized the room had gone silent. There was one female standing there all on her own. The fifth male had not arrived.

Her head was down, humiliation burning her cheeks. I felt sick for her. Oh gods, I wanted to go to her.

I took a stilted step forward—

The sound of boots on the marble floor echoed through the silent room.

"The final member of The Five, their esteemed commander, Constantine Caputo."

A gasp was the only sound that followed that pronouncement.

A huge male closed in, his head dipping as he spoke to the lone female. There was a commotion from the female's parents.

I couldn't hear what was being said, but the uproar ended as fast as it began.

A moment later music began, and Nero led me to the dance floor inside a huge glass-walled sunroom off the main one. The other couples joined us. We were to have one dance, an attempt to make all of this civilized, I guessed, and not like a group of females being handed over to not just strangers but bloodthirsty warriors who were taking us away from everything we knew.

Nero held me to him, his icy stare demanding my attention. He towered over me as power and strength rolled off him. He was a monster in a really bad disguise.

I suspected the other females on this dance floor had dreamed of this day, had built it up to something wonderfully magical. They'd had five years to fantasize about their escape from the confinement of their homes, romanticizing what their mate would be like. I'd had five years of dread.

Whatever lay ahead for me, my only consolation was I would no longer be a prisoner in my own home. I could live my life. Yes, I would belong to this terrifying male, but there was no longer any need to keep me hidden away. I could endure whatever came next as long as I was finally allowed some freedom.

He dipped his head. "Your fear, I can feel it, smell it."

"And you like that, don't you?" I said, even though I knew I shouldn't. I'd never been good at holding my temper, but what did he expect? This male had repeatedly hurt me.

"Oh yes. It's intoxicating," Nero said, low, with no inflection in his voice. "I can't wait to taste it."

A shudder moved through me. There was no kindness buried deep in his heart, no hidden depths reserved for only me. No, this male didn't have a heart. I couldn't count on a conscience to guide him. I was about to become the mate of, be at the mercy of a male who felt absolutely nothing. Who felt no pain, who didn't understand empathy, and who held no warmth in his soul.

"You're not the only one with fangs," I said as he glided me easily around the dance floor.

His gaze searched mine. "Do you think you can hurt me, bride?"

I tried to hold his gaze, but it was impossible. Holding that stare turned my blood cold and my bones to liquid. Still, I refused to cower. "I don't know. Maybe."

His head tilted to the side. "I very much hope so, Lalka."

I froze in his arms, but he kept me moving. I wasn't equipped to spar with this male. I didn't understand him or what he wanted from me. I'd never wanted to be back in my awful pink bedroom, locked away and safe, more than in this moment. "What does Lalka mean?" I forced myself to ask.

His gaze darkened. "Doll," he said in a tone that chilled me to the bone.

The song ended, and the dancing stopped as the sunroom roof began to slide back, revealing the blood moon above us. It was huge in the night sky, shining down, bathing us all in its red glow.

I glanced up at Nero, and the coldness had left his face. The stony mask was gone and in its place was the predator, hungry, wild, and about to pounce—to feast.

One by one, the girls were lifted off the ground, their cries of fear and shock spiking terror through me as they were carried from the ballroom.

I shook my head and tried to step back, but it was too late to run now. With a low snarl, Nero snatched me from my feet, lifting me like a rag doll, and tossed me over his shoulder.

My gaze caught my mother's fearful one, and I choked down my scream as he carried me out into the night.

Two

MINA

NERO STRODE THROUGH THE DARKNESS, heading deeper into the garden, then through a narrow opening in the hedgerow.

I squirmed, biting back another scream as he applied pressure against the backs of my thighs and slid me down the front of his body before placing me on my feet.

His violet eyes shone down at me as he backed me up against the hedge. "You know what happens now, don't you, Mina?"

His wide chest was a wall, blocking everything out, everything but him. I swallowed, and the sound was loud in the cocoon he'd ensconced me in. "Yes."

"I can hear the rush of your blood throbbing through your veins."

I wasn't surprised. My heart was pounding furiously in my chest—but I heard nothing from him. I could only assume his blood moved through the arrogant male's veins from the sheer force of his will.

His hand moved fast, one moment down at his side, the next, holding my jaw in a firm grip. He tilted my head to the side, his gaze sliding to my throat.

I held my breath as he dipped lower, closing the small space between us, and pressed his nose to the spot between my shoulder and throat. The air slid shakily from between my lips as he breathed deep, dragging his nose along my skin and up to my jaw. "I've never wanted to taste anything as much as you," he said, voice hoarse. "It's as if the fates put the gods' own ambrosia in your veins just for me."

His touch was cold, but his breath was warm. The juxtaposition had goose bumps lifting all over my skin. There was no way to stop the way I trembled, even as a slow building warmth, a yearning—a familiar ache that I'd experienced before in his presence—steadily grew between my thighs.

He scraped a fang across my skin, and I jumped, a cry of alarm escaping before I could hold it back.

He made a low, animalistic sound, and pressed his cool cheek against mine, his lips brushing my ear. "Are you a witch, little Mina?"

"I—I'm no witch."

"Then what is this spell you've cast over me?" There was another scrape of his fang, and I gasped. "Your warmth, your scent..." he purred. "It's maddening, enthralling."

Someone screamed in the distance, followed by a low moan somewhere else. Oh gods, what was happening to the others? What was happening to me? I was filled with terror, but that desperate ache pulsing through my body continued to intensify.

"I-is that why you kept coming back? Is that why you came to my room even when you knew it hurt me?" I had to know.

He breathed deeply, scenting me again. "When I stood in your pretty pink room while you huddled in your bed, shaking with fear and desperate need, I felt *something*—when I haven't felt anything in a very long time."

His voice was unmoved, as cold as always.

"What did you feel?" I questioned.

"Agony."

A chill slid through me. "And you want that?"

"Yes." His cool lips touched the hinge of my jaw as his hand slid up my back, then unlatched the choker that he'd left in my dressing room for me and slid it in his pocket. "I want a lot of things, Mina. I want to taste your pain, your need, your rage and fear, and I want to know what it is to be loved, adored by my innocent little mate."

What he said, even the way he said it, was twisted, dark, and strangely naive. "You have to know that love isn't just taking, it's giving as well." I knew, because I'd seen it with my parents. "You can't command me to love you. How could I love a male who would revel in my agony and take pleasure from my pain?" I blinked up at him. Yes, I was afraid, terrified, but a being without emotions meant he couldn't be angry with me, he couldn't be disappointed, he wasn't capable of it, so I told him the truth. "You will never know what it feels like to be loved by me, because I could never love a monster like you, Nero."

He stared down at me, unblinking. "How disappointing," he said, but there was no trace of disappointment on his face or in his voice whatsoever.

Before I could reply, he jerked my head to the side, and sunk his fangs deep into my throat. I screamed and tried to jerk back, but his arms banded around me, holding me fast. Warmth slid from the spot where his fangs impaled my flesh, then slid down my neck. His lips were cold, his tongue hot as he sucked heavily on my vein.

Oh gods. I'd stopped fighting. Instead, my hands fisted his shirt at his sides, hanging on, desperate for purchase as my knees threatened to give out. The warmth slid lower—over my chest, behind my ribs, a scorching swirl through my belly—before gripping me between the thighs.

I groaned as my inner muscles turned liquid, clutching and spasming as the ache reached new heights. My underwear was soaked through so thoroughly that my thighs were slippery. I knew the wetness; I'd experienced it during Nero's visits, and the days after. It was shameful, and humiliating, especially with him so close, but I didn't know how to make it stop.

There was no pulling away, though, no hiding from it, because that all-consuming need that he caused in me, grew deeper, more intense until it overrode all thoughts and feelings completely. Without my say-so, I pressed closer to him, and my hips...*oh gods*, my hips rocked, reaching for something, something I couldn't name but had fully possessed me in the seeking of it.

I felt so incredibly empty all of a sudden. "I n-need..." I gasped. "I need..." I growled—confused, hungry, desperate for that unknown dark *thing*, so wrong and wild and animalistic. It was as if Nero had taken full possession of my body, and I had no control of it to speak of.

He snarled roughly as he sucked deeper, wringing a wanton moan from me when I felt it coiling hotly between my thighs. My muscles clenched, drawing up in a way that had me gasping, then holding my breath.

"Don't fight it," he grated against my jaw. "It's mine, Mina, give it to me. Give me what's mine," he said against my skin.

I didn't know what he wanted from me. He was the one with all the control.

My thighs were pressed tightly together, clenching as the muscles inside me clutched desperately at nothing. I was hot, sweating, my body so tense I felt ready to snap any moment as the wild sensation grew higher, so wonderful—yet terrifying. Nero sucked harder on my vein—

I shattered, and a keening wail burst from my lips as it washed over me, feeling like I had been tossed into the deepest ocean during a storm. I had no control over my body or the sounds that came from me, and, oh gods, it felt good, so good that I didn't care.

I didn't care that I gripped Nero's shirt so tight that the fabric was tearing beneath my nails, or about the moans and cries that I couldn't hold back. The only thing I cared about was the feeling rolling through me. That was all that mattered.

My pulse sped frantically as he dragged his tongue over my throat, sealing his bite. Everything clenched again, and the wetness between my legs slid down my inner thigh as the pleasure eased, and I was left limp against him. I tried to cringe and pull away, but he held me there, not giving me an inch.

My face was scalding with humiliation from the way I'd reacted, at the way my body had responded to his touch.

"You are the most delicious morsel I have ever tasted," he said, his voice now hoarse. "Will my blood be as delicious to you, do you think?" He squeezed my hip and tilted his head back as he breathed in deep again, scenting me. "With how wet you are, I think you'll come again from just a taste—" He stilled, and lifted his head, on full alert.

"What is it?"

"We need to go."

A commotion came from somewhere deeper in the garden. I had no chance to ask anything else, because Nero suddenly lifted me into his arms, threw me over his shoulder, and ran. So fast, the world around me was a blur.

When he finally stopped, it was to put me in the back seat of a car.

A moment later we sped away.

I spun to him. "What just happened?"

"Shots were fired." He stared over at me. "One of the females' fathers had a change of heart." His gaze darkened. "He has to know there is no taking her back. There is no taking any of you back." He licked his lower lip. It was fuller, darker after feeding. "You belong to me now, Mina. Every part of you is mine."

I stared at him—the arrogant and extremely old vampire I was tied to for eternity—and my stomach cramped from the finality of those words.

I was no match for a male like him, but I wouldn't, couldn't, roll over and not at least fight for myself. "If I belong to you...then you belong to me."

His violet eyes seemed to brighten in the darkness of the cab. "You want to own me?" His gaze searched mine. "You wouldn't know what to do with me, little doll," he finally said, then looked ahead, going still once again, as if he were made of marble.

I sat there not sure what to say, what to do. So I did nothing, said nothing. I simply sat there in my embarrassingly wet underwear, my stomach making sounds that gave away how deep my hunger was as we drove through the city.

Finally, we drove down an alleyway and parked behind a huge concrete building. Nero climbed out, rounded the car, and opened my door, while his driver unloaded my bags from the trunk.

Nero's cold hand curled around mine, and he led me to the back of the building, punched numbers into a keypad by the door, then led me through. We walked into a dark hallway with doors branching off it.

"What is this place?"

"Your new home," he said without inflection as he led me briskly down the windowless hallway.

"Where are we going?"

He stopped in front of a door. "We need to complete the binding before the blood moon goes down."

I swallowed thickly—I had to drink from him.

He pushed the door open. It was dark inside, but the glow of the moon leaked around the edges of the curtains and gave the walls around it a pinky tinge. He led me across the room without turning on the light. My heart sped frantically and my mouth went dry as that humiliating ache between my thighs started to build again.

He sat in a wide armchair, thighs spread, his fingers loosely curled around the arms, and I stood there in front of him not sure what to do.

"Have you ever fed this way before, Mina?"

I shook my head. "As per the rules of a claimed female, I was given blood from a glass, from different donors." Drinking from one person regularly risked a bond forming. When a female turned sixteen, they developed their need to feed. Because I'd already been claimed by Nero, I wasn't permitted to ever feed directly from a vein. When I did do it the first time, it would only be from my mate—from the cold male watching me now.

"Have you fantasized about it?" he asked. "About sinking those little fangs into someone?"

His violet eyes were locked on me, as if he could see into my soul. "Yes," I whispered, unable to lie. I wanted to taste him, this terrifying, ice-cold male. Despite everything, I wanted to know how his blood would feel sliding over my tongue and down my throat.

"Come here, then," he said.

I blinked down at him. "Where?" There was no room. He took up the entire chair.

His hand moved so fast, it was only a flash in the darkness. His cool fingers curled around my wrist, and he tugged me forward, knocking me off-balance, then snatched me off my feet and planted me on his lap.

My face instantly burned. "What are you doing?"

"You can't feed all the way over there, now can you?"

I didn't know where to put my hands, so curled them in my lap.

"Don't act coy," he said as he slid the choker from his pocket and secured it around my throat. The weight was heavy, again like he'd curled his fingers around my throat and kept them there. "The last time I saw you, you were anything but."

I was trembling now, in frustration and anger that this male was my mate. That the fates chose this cruel male to be mine. "I don't know what to do."

"Yes, you do," he said. "You're a vampire, Mina. Take it. Take what's yours or lose it. Time is running out."

If I didn't drink before the sun went down, if I didn't do this now, I would go home in disgrace. I would shame my family. I'd be mateless for the rest of my long life. I turned to him in the darkness. There was no warmth radiating from him, not in any definition of the word. As a little girl, I dreamed of a male who would love me, care for me—not this cold, heartless monster.

Many old vampires lost the ability to feel emotion. Those who had never found their mates, who had never fallen in love were unable to retain or regain the ability to *feel*, stuck for eternity like the cold creature beneath me.

He hadn't always been this way, though, I reminded myself. I had to have faith. I had to believe the fates knew what they were doing when they chose this male for me. Faith was all I had right then. Love had been powerful enough to bring back the emotions of vampires as old and cold as Nero. My mother had told me the stories, like fairy tales told to me when I was little, but still the truth. It had happened before. I had to believe it could happen for us.

Can you ever love him, though?

I honestly didn't know, but despite what I said to him, I had to try. I had to try to make this work, for both our sakes.

"Mina," he said, and there was actual urgency in his deep voice this time.

The moon was going down, I felt it as well, humming through my body as if it were calling out to me. Nero felt it just as strongly, and that urgency told me so. He wanted this. He wanted me. He may not admit how much, he may not even know or understand what he was feeling in this moment, but he did want this.

That knowledge empowered me in a way I'd never experienced before. He told me to take what was mine. Then that's what I'd do. My fangs tingled and my stomach growled as a part of me I'd held back roared forward.

"Mina," he snapped.

I grabbed his jaw, jerked his head to the side, and struck. Blood instantly flooded my mouth, rich and fragrant, the most delicious blood I'd ever tasted. He grabbed the back of my neck, his fingers curling in, gripping tight. He was going to pull me off him. I snarled before I knew I was doing it, digging my nails into his flesh to hold on, lost to his taste, his scent, becoming the base creature I truly was.

"I'm not going to stop you," he said roughly. "Drink your fill, little doll."

I needed more, wanted more. My body was hot and achy. I had to get closer. As if he could read my mind, he shifted me on his lap until I straddled him. It was indecent, but I didn't care. There was something hard beneath me, and when it made contact with the slick, throbbing part of me, it felt wonderful, and I moaned against his throat.

His hand slid up and down my spine. "That's it. Use me to slake your needs. Fill your belly and rub that little virgin cunt on me."

I didn't know that word, but I didn't need to in order to understand what it meant. I ground against the hard thing digging into me, chasing the feeling that was building fast inside me, coiling between my thighs and in my lower belly, making my muscles quiver, while I sucked greedily on his vein. It was the same feeling I'd had in the garden when Nero had fed from me, but more intense because I could rub and grind and roll my hips, chasing the pressure I needed.

Then it hit me with force, not a wave this time but a brick wall of pleasure slamming into me. I tore my mouth away, a scream bursting forth as my inner muscles clamped down on nothing, squeezing and clutching desperately. I rode it out, until it finally eased.

Panting, I fell forward, my face against his shoulder.

"Seal your bite," Nero said, his voice back to a cold void.

I could barely move, but I lifted my hand to the opposite side of his throat and pulled myself closer so I could lazily drag my tongue over the puncture marks I'd made in his skin. The marks vanished, healing almost instantly, not because my saliva was particularly powerful but because he was so old and strong.

He stood then, with me in his arms, and walked to the bed. "Are we going to mate now?" I asked drowsily.

"No."

He placed me on a bed, the room so dark I couldn't see much, but I felt him place a blanket over me. I was full and drowsy and content in a way I never had been in my life. Gods, it should be impossible, but I felt close to him. To the male who had tormented me on the eve of my birthday for years.

He headed for the door.

"Nero?"

"Yes?"

"Where are you going?"

"My room."

Disappointment filled me. "You don't want to...stay here with me?"

"This is where you belong, Lalka, my little doll. Only you." Then he walked out, shutting the door behind him.

Three

MINA

MY EYES WERE hot and gritty as I yawned and stretched. I still had on my dress from the ceremony, and my limbs felt all loose, and...*mmm*...really nice. Rolling to my side, I opened my eyes.

I blinked as my heart slammed so hard into the back of my ribs that my lungs emptied on a sudden burst. *No.* I shook my head, trying to clear it.

I didn't understand. Had I dreamed it? All of it?

I shoved back the quilt and lunged from the bed. Sprinting to the window, I threw back the curtains and gasped. A cement block wall was several yards from my window. I wasn't back home. This wasn't the view from my childhood bedroom.

I turned back, taking in the entire room again, from the sheer pale-pink lace that hung behind the curtains to the cotton candy–colored quilt and throw pillows, to the fluffy fuchsia rug beside the bed—it was the same. It was all the same.

Every piece of furniture: the walnut dresser and side tables. The salmon desk beside the window that matched the walls. The wide pink-and-white striped armchair, the one Nero had sat in last night while I'd fed from him—it was all *exactly* the same.

I pressed my hand to my stomach when it clenched violently.

Oh gods. What the hell was this? Why had Nero done this? I rushed to the door, gripping the handle, turning it, yanking it, but it was locked. I was locked in.

He'd locked me in!

I paced away and back, then tried it again, and again, but there was no getting out. Panic choked me, and I pounded on the door as hard as I could. "Let me out!" I screamed the words over and over until my throat was raw.

Stumbling back, I finally collapsed on the floor, the layers of my pink tulle dress puffing out all around me. I ran a shaky finger over a drop of dried blood on the skirt, Nero's blood. My bonded had locked me in here.

The sound of the lock turning echoed through the door, and I lifted my head as it opened, swiping the tears from my cheeks as Nero walked in and shut the door behind him.

He stared down, regarding me impassively. "What are you doing on the floor, Mina?"

"Why did you lock me in here?" I wanted him to tell me something, anything, that made a liar of the voice roaring in my head.

His gaze slid over my face, and the intensity of it made me want to squirm. I quickly climbed to my feet, not wanting to be so weak, so vulnerable in front of him, and his gaze continued down my body in a way that lifted goose bumps all over me.

Finally, his violet eyes slid back to mine. "Feeding from me has altered your appearance. Your cheeks are pink and your lips are like rubies. Your blond hair shines and your lavender eyes are much brighter."

Was he trying to pay me a compliment? "I...uh...thank you. But you haven't answered my question." I crossed my arms. "Why did you lock me in here, and...why am I in a replica of my bedroom?"

"Standing there in your pink dress, in this pink room, you look like a little doll," he said, again not answering my question.

He called me that, he'd called me little doll several times now. It didn't feel like a compliment. And I didn't like it. Not at all. "And that's what you want?"

His head tilted to the side in a way that was all predator. "Is it not what you want?"

"To be locked in this room? To be held prisoner in a twisted replica of my childhood bedroom?" I stared at him in shocked horror. "Of course not. Why would I want this?"

"What did you think would happen?" he asked, and I thought I might detect a touch of genuine curiosity in his voice.

"I don't know...definitely not this." I chewed my lip, trying to think, to come up with a way to get through to him. "My mother said... She said that we would...that you would..."

"What?"

Humiliation burned my face. "That we would mate after we fed from each other. I assumed that's what we would do." Then afterward I would finally have some freedom.

He closed the space between us and dispassionately swiped a tear from my cheek. "And you want that? Why?"

"I don't, but the fates chose us for each other, right? There has to be a reason for that. I have to believe there's a reason for that, for this...this..." I bit my lips together.

"What? What is this?"

My pulse was frantic, but I couldn't hold the words back. "A nightmare."

He studied me. "I've given you everything you could want. All your favorite things. Your books, your clothes, all your most treasured possessions, little doll. I believe after you have recovered from the shock, you'll grow to enjoy your life here."

"Here? In this room?"

"Yes."

"This is where you belong, Lalka, my little doll. Only you."

His words from the night before came back to me. He liked me here. He'd visited me in my room, every birthday from the age of sixteen because he'd gotten some kind of twisted gratification from it.

I didn't know what that was, but it was enough that he'd wanted to recreate it. I was a...a thing, an object. An amusement.

He'd created a doll's house for me, his little doll, trapped so he could watch me, enjoying my pain and fear while I pounded against the door, desperate for release. The freedom I longed for would never be mine. I'd left one prison, only to be taken to another.

"This is twisted, Nero. You have to know that?"

"Is it?" he said, but he didn't want an answer. He didn't care. He curled his fingers around the side of my throat, his thumb pressing against my wildly fluttering pulse. "You'll get used to it, Lalka."

We weren't mated, but we were blood bound, which meant for me the suffering he'd caused me with every one of his visits was over. But if we remained unmated, he would be the one to suffer, he had to know that.

Maybe I should hold my tongue, this male was so incredibly cold, capable of anything, but right then I couldn't think of anything worse than the circumstances I found myself in now, so I didn't hold back. I let the temper that my parents often scolded me for loose. "And you'll need to get used to the pain I promised you," I said. "You don't want me as your mate? Fine. Just know that when the pain is more than you can bear, and you're begging for me to take it away, I won't. I wouldn't mate with you now even if my life depends on it. You don't want me? No, Nero. I won't have you."

The muscle in his jaw tightened. "Is that right?"

"Yes, and just so you know, I will find a way out of here. I will leave you, and I'll never come back," I fired at him, then gave him my back and walked to the window, staring at the brick wall across from me.

I sounded like a child throwing a tantrum, but it was all I had.

Rejecting him, when he'd already rejected me, was the only weapon I possessed.

The sound of the door closing, the lock engaging a moment later, had me spinning around.

A highly ineffective weapon.

He'd left without a word.

How could you wound when your target was incapable of feeling pain?

I didn't see Nero for two days after that. A male who said little, named Pretender—an odd name, if you asked me—brought me food.

No, I hadn't been in here that long, but I already felt as if I were losing my mind.

My only escape was when I slept. I climbed into bed now and turned off the lamp. Then I stared at the ceiling because I didn't even have anything new to read. All the books on the bookshelf were identical to the ones I'd had in my bedroom at home, all books I'd already read. He truly thought of me like some kind of doll frozen in time and space. As if I didn't exist outside of his yearly visits.

I'd never encountered anyone like him, which wasn't so surprising, I suppose, considering I'd been locked away for the last five years, but still, I'd met old vampires before. None of them had been as twisted as Nero.

The sound of the lock turning, slowly, carefully, reached me in the darkness, and I held my breath. I knew it was him, instantly. I gripped the covers, about to jump out of bed, but then froze as the door slowly and silently swung open.

I kept my eyes closed, waiting, listening, while I felt his gaze burning into me. Had he changed his mind? Had he realized he'd made a mistake and he wanted me to be his mate, after all? Did I even want that anymore?

Anything has to be better than the situation I'm in now.

But the silence dragged on. He made no move to come closer, and he said nothing. He just stood and watched me like he had the times before at my parents' house.

He hadn't changed his mind.

He hadn't come for me, he'd come for whatever it was he got out of being this close to me. This room, my prison, it was all about recreating his past visits. Only this time, I wasn't suffering, there was no *intoxicating* pain for him to revel in.

There was fear, though. So much of it. I was confused, alone, and now that I had a taste of just how disturbed Nero truly was, the fear was deeper than ever before.

He wanted that, didn't he? He wanted me to be a good little doll, to lie in my bed, squirming and afraid, to feed the ravenous beast inside him delicious morsels of my terror.

Well, I refused to just lie here. Despite how afraid I was, I wouldn't give him permission to treat me this way. I wouldn't play along with this...this twisted fantasy of his.

Taking a steadying breath, I opened my eyes and lifted to my elbows. His violet eyes glowed in the darkness and locked on to mine.

"Lie back down, Mina. Close your eyes," he said, his voice strange, tight.

I forced myself to stare back. "No, I won't do it."

He moved quick, so fast, I didn't see him coming. One moment he stood across the room, the next he was leaning over me.

"You belong to me, little doll. You do as I command."

"I will not." That's when I noticed the strain on his face. "You're in pain."

He bared his teeth and leaned closer, his lips just a breath from mine. "Yes," he said softly. "Do you know how long it's been since I've felt true agony, Mina? Since I've felt deep satisfying pleasure?"

I shook my head, my breath shaking.

"Centuries." He licked his lips. "I got only a small taste of it, just once a year, when I allowed myself to visit you, but that was nothing compared to this." He hissed low, and it morphed into a low groan. "Nothing like this."

Oh gods, he liked it. He liked the pain. But maybe after centuries of nothing, of feeling absolutely nothing at all, even pain would be welcome?

For a moment, just a second, I actually felt sorry for him. I shoved the feeling down, because how I handled this situation would dictate how he treated me in the future. Or maybe it would have no effect on him at all. How could a man who hadn't felt anything emotionally and, by the sounds of it, physically for centuries understand that what he was doing, how he was treating me, hurt? That it was causing the kind of damage between us that could never be repaired. That if he had a change of heart, that if he decided he wanted more from me, that I might never be able to forgive him?

It seemed impossible, but I had to try. I had to try to understand him, to make him understand me.

I looked up at him, still so close. "You don't enjoy feeding? It doesn't make you feel good."

His gaze dipped to my throat. "It had ceased to..." The tip of his tongue peeked out, sliding along the seam of his lips. "Until I tasted you under the blood moon."

I nodded slowly, trying to decide the best way to say what I wanted to say. It was hard to think with him so close, with his massive body looming over me like a starved predator. I struggled to get the words right. "Don't you want to keep experiencing that? Don't you want more? To feel more? If you let me out, if we spent time togeth—"

"No, little doll, this is enough."

I glared back at him. "I don't believe you."

"Lying would require me to care about your thoughts and feelings on the matter. I'm incapable of that. Whatever romantic notions you're carrying around in your head, you need to squash them. This is where you'll stay because this is where I want you to be. This is all I will ever want from you."

My fear twisted with anger as it reared up inside me. "Well, this is not enough *for me*, Nero. How could this ever be enough for anyone?"

"These are your new circumstances. You need to get used to them." He brushed my hair back from my face. "And from now on when I come into your room at night, you will lie still and silent, do you understand?"

He couldn't be serious. "No. I won't—"

His fingers slipped around my throat, not tight but with enough pressure to shut me up. "I have been very accommodating, Mina. I'm not known for my kindness or my patience."

True paralyzing fear gripped me as I looked into his icy gaze, followed by a wave of complete and utter hopelessness.

"If there is anything you need, ask Pretender and he will get it for you. When you need to feed, tell him, and I will come to you during the day...but at night, when I am in this room, you do not speak, and you do not move, do you understand?"

I was frozen in place.

"Nod, Mina. Nod that you understand what your bonded requires of you."

It was hard, but somehow I managed it.

His eyes glittered, his fingers slipping away, finally releasing me, then he walked out, locking the door behind him.

Four

NERO

I LOOKED DOWN at the packed dance floor below, muted music reaching me through the large window in my office. The humans who frequented The Bank were oblivious to who and what they were dancing with, who they would take home and fuck later that night. I didn't care what happened to them when they left my club, why would I? I didn't care about anything, and I didn't dwell on things, but for some reason I couldn't stop thinking about her.

My little doll in her pretty room below ground.

I had grown so numb to my own instincts, so disconnected to all but the need to occasionally feed that this new sensation inside me, the one that drove me to seek her out, was all-consuming. It was primal, built into the fabric of our being, and part of what made us vampire, but it had been buried deep inside me under layers of ice. Until now. The force of it was a shock to the system, pumping life back to the withered and cold places that had been long forgotten, and I hadn't decided if this partial reanimation was unwelcome or not.

I craved the pain that being near Mina gave me, but now, even when I wasn't with her, it remained a constant ache inside me—and so was my thirst for her.

Drinking, fucking had both been biological needs that I fulfilled when necessary. I didn't need to feed often, not anymore; it had become a tasteless, joyless endeavor. Fucking, much the same.

The last time I was inside a female was in The Vault, the feeding club I owned just below this one, and I'd felt nothing. The encounter happened a short time after I found Mina, after I stood at her window and felt the incredible pull that I recognized instantly.

I hadn't sought out a bedmate since.

And now that I'd tasted my little Lalka in the garden, I'd been, hungry for her, off-balance, ever since.

Draining the bourbon from my glass, I strode to the door on the other side of my office and took the private hall, then down the stairs to my basement apartment. Opening the door at the bottom, I kept walking. Mina's room was only a few doors down, but I refused to let base instinct take over. Instead of going to her, I used my key and entered The Vault through my private access, rounded the faux wall in the darkened corner, and strode into the feeding club.

The scent of sex and blood filled my senses instantly, heavy and rich, and for the first time since I opened this club, the smell actually turned my stomach. Ignoring the churning inside me and the fawning donors watching me as I strode across the floor, I took my place at my usual table.

Pretender appeared at my side a moment later with another glass of bourbon, then stayed there to stop anyone who might think to approach me.

"Did she eat today?" I asked him. My stubborn bonded hadn't eaten in three days, not since I told her what I wanted from her.

Pretender shook his head under his hooded sweatshirt. "She's still refusing."

"Did she say why?"

He didn't meet my eyes, but I could see his glittering. "She said she'd rather starve to death than live in a prison."

My ward was concerned. I knew that look on his face well.

"You believe her?"

He shrugged a shoulder. "I believe she believes it. I don't think she'll hold out forever, but I could hear her stomach growling."

I sipped my drink. "She'll give in soon enough."

Pretender nodded, but the way he was unable to stay still told me there was something more he wanted to say.

"What is it?" I said.

He looked uncomfortable. "I'm of course not telling you I know best. I know nothing about these matters, but I do know young vampires like her, new to feeding from the vein and newly bonded, need to feed much more often. She'll waste a lot faster than, for example, I would." His gaze came to me. "You may have forgotten what it's like to be truly hungry."

He was right. I had. Until Mina, I hadn't been hungry in longer than I could remember. I knew when I needed to feed, and I fed, but there'd been no pleasure in it. No urgency. "You think she's wasting already?"

He shrugged. "She looked thinner than the first time I saw her. I don't think it's developed beyond that, but I can see the affects her refusal to eat or feed is having on her."

Stubborn little fool.

I should have thought of it, of course. It was her age, her new situation. "I told her to tell you if she needed to feed."

Pretender chewed his lip. "I don't think her pride will allow it."

I curled my fingers tighter around my glass. Her behavior was illogical. Death was far worse than living in the comfortable room I'd provided for her. I'd painstakingly recreated it. It had taken years to get it just right, to make it a perfect replica, and she would rather die than be in it?

A strange sensation burned in the center of my chest.

I stood abruptly, then strode back through the room, leaving the club through my private access and back out into the hall.

For centuries, there'd been nothing that I wanted or needed. Nothing drew my eye or held my attention. Nothing made me feel.

Until my little doll.

I'd visited her room every night since I'd brought her here, and besides that one night, she'd lain still, silent like I'd asked, while I watched her, while I basked in what only she could give me. The pain she caused in me, the hunger, had awoken something inside me that I thought I'd lost forever. I would not lose that, not now.

Mina would not give up and waste away. I wouldn't let her do that to me.

I would not let her take this from me.

Removing the key from my pocket, I unlocked her door and walked into her room. She wasn't in her bed and, for a moment before I saw her on the other side of the room, a strange and sharp feeling stabbed through my gut.

She sat in the chair by the window. The city lights that had managed to reach her through the window made the side of her face look pale and her blond hair impossibly glossy. She was wearing one of the dresses from her closet, not the gown she'd been wearing at the ceremony but a different one.

They were all pink and lacy, modest. I liked seeing her like that, untainted by the outside world—innocent, safe. She had her arms wrapped around her drawn-up knees, the fabric of her gown hanging almost to the floor. Her head was slightly turned, staring out at nothing.

"Look at me, Mina," I said, my voice oddly rough.

"Why?" she said, though it was barely a whisper.

Why was she doing this? "Because your bonded has asked you to."

"Yeah? Well, your bonded wants you to let her the hell out of this room, but that's not going to happen. Get used to the disappointment. I have."

I wasn't sure what to do, what to say. When I gave an order, it was obeyed, always. Closing the space between us, I took her chin in my hand. I needed her eyes on me, for some reason. I needed my little doll to look at me. She let me turn her head my way, but she kept her eyes averted, refusing to give me what I wanted as if she knew how desperately I needed it.

"Look at me," I said, and it came out an animal growl, my voice so different, I barely recognized it.

Her lashes fluttered, but still she refused.

I gripped her chin harder, and she winced. I quickly let go. I didn't like that, either, that wince of pain. "Mina," I said again.

Still she gave me nothing.

"Why are you behaving this way?"

She turned back to the window, looking out at the concrete wall across from it. I stared down at her while the thump of her racing heart throbbed through me. She wasn't afraid, not really, there was something else. I didn't know what she was feeling. It tasted bitter like fear, but there was more to it.

"You need to eat, and you need to feed," I said into the silence. "I demand you stop this."

Still, she gave me nothing.

She was hungry, I could hear it, and I could already see how her lack of sustenance of any kind for the last three days had affected her. Her shoulders looked narrower, her wrists and arms thinner.

Being this close to her had my own pain radiating through my body. It was sweet, an intoxicating agony, and it increased daily, worsening when I was close to her like this, and staying away was becoming much more difficult.

Every instinct roared at me to snatch her from her seat, to force her to feed, to fuck my stubborn bride, to claim what was mine, to *mate*, but I wasn't sure I could survive such an onslaught of sensation and come away with my sanity intact. I'd gone too long without emotion, without true pleasure. There was a real chance I would kill her if I gave in to the force of need that burned inside me.

There was a real chance that if I did give in, if I allowed myself to have her, I would tear her apart, glutting on her in every conceivable way until there was nothing left.

For the longest time, I'd convinced myself I was glad I felt nothing, but now...now she was here, I felt a shift inside me, and I wasn't so sure anymore. All I knew was if I let my control slip, even a little, I could lose her.

I hadn't wanted anything, not like this, in a very long time, and I wanted to keep her, which meant I couldn't let her die, not by my hand or hers.

Not knowing what else to do, I sunk my fangs into my wrist and held it in front of her mouth. She jerked away, pressing back into the chair, trying to escape my blood as it dripped onto her pink gown. "Drink," I ordered.

She turned away completely when I held my wrist closer. I gripped the back of her head and held my wrist to her tightly clamped lips. Mina thrashed wildly, exploding from the chair, and dragged the back of her hand across her mouth, wiping away my blood. Her eyes flashed and I felt her fury. She ran to the bathroom, slamming and locking the door after her.

I strode up to it, gripping the handle. It was impossibly hard to hold back, but I didn't turn it. Gritting my teeth, I wrestled down the sensations flowing over me, through me. It was dangerous, what I was feeling, I recognized that much. I could easily break through the door, hold her down, force her mouth open, and make her drink.

But I wouldn't stop there. I knew that after I fed her, I would feast on her, on her blood, on her cunt. I'd take and take. I would break her down and tear her apart until there was only a bloody shell of my little Lalka left.

So instead, I forced myself to release the door handle and retreat before I did something I couldn't take back.

Five

NERO

Hours later, I was still pacing outside Mina's door.

I'd left her room, but I couldn't walk away.

I could smell her.

I could hear her breathing and the rush of her blood—the growls of her empty stomach.

The look on her face, her downcast eyes, the way she'd fled to the bathroom to escape me had been repeating over and over in my mind.

I felt as feral as I had as a young male. So out of control, I'd been brought in by our elders, recruiters of The Five, and given a choice: train under them or be put to death. The wild thing I'd been had been molded into a calculated predator, unmatched by any other in our race for my ability to track, hunt, and kill. I became The Five's assassin, the monster they sent in when the most difficult to reach of our enemies needed to be exterminated.

Tonight, the cold, calculated predator was gone, and only the wild thing remained. I couldn't stop myself from reaching for the handle and gripping it tight. It took everything in me, but somehow I wrestled back the slavering monster inside me as I opened her door for the second time that night with a low growl.

The room was dark now, but the darkness was no barrier for me. I could see everything as if it were daylight. Mina was in bed. She lay on her side, her blond hair spread across her pillow. Yes, her face was thinner now, but her lips looked darker, her cheeks pink.

She'd refused my blood, but a little had touched her lips. That pink in her cheeks, the darker shade of her lips, told me she'd lapped up at least a small amount when she'd run into the bathroom.

Her dress was on the floor, and I picked it up. The drops that had landed on the skirt were now pale smears, almost gone completely. I scented it, and that strange sensation in my chest pinched with pain when I realized she'd sucked the fabric almost clean, desperate for my blood despite her refusals. The pain was different now, and it lingered behind my ribs. I didn't like this pain. I took no pleasure from it.

I should stay where I was, for her own protection, but my feet carried me to her bedside. She was asleep, not pretending. Her lashes twitched, and she was breathing erratically. I scented her again, and the mouthwatering perfume of her cunt hit me in the gut, making my cock ache as deeply as the rest of my body.

A being was most vulnerable while they slept. Between the moments of sleep and wake, those mere seconds between the two, in that fog of confusion, your mind played tricks on you, your guard dropped, and instinct took over completely—especially for a young vampire like my Lalka.

Nicking my wrist, I held it in front of her nose. Her lips parted on a groan, and I swiped my finger gently over her cheek. "Lalka."

Her eyes snapped open, wide, locking on mine. The instant relief that I *felt*, that those lavender eyes were finally on me again, was instant. Her gaze was dazed, disorientated, and before her brain had time to process what was happening, her instinct took over as expected. Her hands shot out of the covers, grabbing my arm, and her little fangs extended a moment before she struck, sinking them into my vein and taking a desperate suck.

My cock pulsed so fucking hard, I almost came, and with each deep draw of my blood, her pull on my vein grew more forceful. I felt each one along my shaft, as if she were sucking it hard. As if those full crimson lips were wrapped around me as desperate for my seed as she was for my blood.

I needed to get closer to her, so I sat on the side of the bed. "That's it, Mina, drink your fill," I said, then for some reason, brushed her pale hair back from her fevered cheek.

She was perspiring and writhing under the covers until, finally, she tossed them back, then kicked the quilt off completely. She wore only her underwear, as if she'd stripped from her dress and stumbled straight into bed. Her thin frame and starved body began to fill out, her pale skin turning pink, her body ripening before my eyes.

Her hips and belly rounded, growing softer, her thighs thicker as they rubbed and pressed together. Her panties were drenched and plastered to her flesh, outlining her pretty untouched pussy. My mouth watered, my cock was so hard and hot, the need inside me gnawed wider, growing more forceful. I dragged in an unneeded breath, filling my lungs with more of her scent. I had never felt desire like this before. It was too much all at once. If I didn't touch her soon, I'd succumb to insanity.

As if my bonded read my mind, she spread her legs and arched. My gaze slid to her lovely face. Her eyes were on me, wide and pleading, while she continued to suck greedily.

"Do you want me to make the ache go away, little doll?"

Her eyes were hot, as wild as I felt when she nodded.

"I'll need to touch you."

She nodded again.

Keeping my eyes on hers, I gently tore her panties from her body, and as soon as the cool air hit her swollen, slick cunt, her lids fluttered and my shameless little doll spread wider for me.

The instinct to mate had taken her over completely. Her body knew what she needed even if Mina didn't understand it. If I'd been a lesser male, weaker, there would be no resisting what she offered in that moment, but something else roared just as loud inside me, something I couldn't name right then, but was strong enough to stop the wild thing I was inside from taking what was mine.

From glutting on her.

From breaking her completely.

Dragging my hand down her soft belly, I finally allowed myself to touch what was mine. Mina groaned as soon as I cupped her dripping pussy. I held her gaze while I dragged the pad of my thumb along the smooth seam, up and back before going deeper. I grazed her clit, and her hips lifted again, while she sobbed against my wrist.

"That feels good, doesn't it?" I rubbed softly over her clit again. "Have you ever touched this part of your body, Mina?"

She shook her head, her cheeks a deep pink.

A rough, rusty sound fell from my lips. It was gritty and dark, and her eyes widened. I couldn't remember the last time I'd laughed, and it surprised us both. "I don't believe you. Inquisitive, feisty little creature you are. Being told no would have only made you more curious." I swiped again. "Did it feel this good when you touched yourself?"

She shook her head, not even trying to deny it now.

"Did you ever make yourself come, little doll?" I could tell by the look in her eyes, she didn't know what I was asking. "What happened to you in the garden the first time you tasted my blood."

She whimpered and shook her head again.

"You need that again now, don't you?"

Another nod, this one subtler, but the way she lifted her hips, seeking more of my touch wasn't.

I needed to make her come, and fast. I needed to leave this room before I got lost in all that she'd awoken in me. Before my control shattered and I accidentally killed her.

Swiping my thumb over her tight opening, I gathered her

juices and continued to tease her clit. Her fangs released me, and she arched back, thrusting her breasts in the air while her thighs trembled.

My blood coated her lips, dripping down her chin, and the sight nearly undid me. A snarl slipped free as she lifted her arms and gripped the headboard, straining and rocking against my hand, her hips moving like they would if I was fucking her.

"Nero?" she gasped out, a question, a plea, it was all there in the sound of my name falling from her lips.

Blood still slid from her bite in my wrist, and I let it run down over my hand and along my finger, then held it above that incredibly tempting mouth. A drop landed between her parted lips, and she grabbed my wrist, pulling it closer. Her tongue flicked out, then she drew my blood-coated finger into her mouth, sucking and licking and moaning, while she writhed like the wanton little creature she was for me.

I felt every suck, every one of those licks along my engorged shaft, as if that lovely mouth was wrapped around my cock.

Her hips rocked frantically now, her skin flushed, body quivering, while she sucked on my finger, desperately lapping up my blood. I'd never seen anything as exquisite as my bride chasing her orgasm.

"Let go," I said through gritted teeth, because I desperately needed it as well, probably more than even she did in that moment. "Give me what I want, Mina."

She moaned and moved faster, and I leaned in so I could get close, so I could watch her, so I didn't miss a thing.

Mina screamed, alarm blending with pleasure, and when her eyes opened, I saw the same. My cock wept at the mix of fear and lust in her eyes, and the way it made my little doll come even harder. My lips peeled back, my fangs elongating as a vicious snarl burst from me, surprising us both, and causing a frisson of strong emotions inside her, sending her high again. I watched the way her pussy clutched around nothing, desperate to be filled, before she crashed back down with a broken moan, coating my fingers and soaking the sheets.

Panting, she stared up at me, watching as I lifted my wrist and dragged my tongue over her puncture marks, sealing the bite before sucking the fingers of my other hand into my mouth, tasting her cunt the only way I could allow myself to.

The daze of satisfaction slipped from her eyes as reality set in. "No, little doll, this was no dream."

She shoved herself back, yanking up the sheet to cover herself, trying to put distance between us, but there was nowhere for her to go. She swallowed convulsively. "You tricked me," she accused. "You—"

"I did what needed to be done. You don't get to starve yourself to death, Mina. I won't allow it."

Fury filled her lavender eyes. "Don't ever do that again," she said, voice shaking. "I never would have... I wouldn't have let you..." Her face darkened.

"You're a vampire. Rejecting your base instincts will only end in you losing control and hurting someone."

"Good, then maybe I'll hurt you."

I stood, sliding my hands into my pockets. "You can't hurt me, little doll, that's impossible."

"I don't want you to touch me, and I don't want your blood," she all but snarled.

I tilted my head to the side, studying her. "We both know that's a lie, now don't we? The soaked sheets you're lying in more than prove that. You crave both, but if you insist on being stubborn, you can go back to feeding from a glass. I'll have Pretender bring you my blood with breakfast." She should always feed from me, I realized in that moment. I wanted her to feed from me, only me, straight from my vein every fucking time, but Mina wouldn't have me, not willingly.

She was breathing hard, her chest heaving with her outraged

breaths, and her cheeks burned with what I assumed was embarrassment. "Are you finished?" she bit out.

"Are you, Lalka?" My gaze dipped to her tempting lips. How did just the sight of them drive my need for her even higher? "Your scent tells me you're not nearly done."

"Get out," she hissed. "Get the hell out of my room."

I inclined my head.

"I hate you!" she yelled as I shut the door behind me, and something crashed against the wooden surface.

Hate was the closest thing to love a being could feel, but to me, muted and cold as I'd been for so long, the sensation of all that emotion rolling off my bride and slamming into me was exhilarating. I didn't care what caused it. I just wanted more of it. Hate was more than fine with me.

Six

MINA

PRETENDER GATHERED up the dishes left from my dinner. The vampire didn't talk much, at least not to me, but he gave me a nod of approval when he picked up my empty glass.

I'd barely stopped myself from running a finger along the inside of it to get every last drop of Nero's blood. It'd still been warm when Pretender brought it in, and I'd been craving more of it since the glass I'd had earlier at breakfast. Who was I kidding. I couldn't stop thinking about drinking straight from Nero's vein.

His blood was so rich and smooth, gods, addicting. I'd never had blood like it. It warmed my belly and between my thighs and zinged through my veins. Too bad the male it came from was cold, sadistic, and completely deranged.

Three days had passed since Nero had tricked me into feeding from him. Nothing had changed for me, my circumstances were the same, but I wasn't sure giving up and wasting away to escape this hell was an option anymore, not with the way I craved Nero's blood. And after what he did to bend me to his will, he'd never let me, even if I tried.

Images flashed through my mind, and the burn of humiliation washed over me again when I thought about the way I'd behaved

—about what I begged him to do to me. My bonded was cruel and selfish and twisted, and still I'd begged for him to touch me. Thanks to fate, I craved that monster; I craved him just like he said I did. He'd seen right through me so easily.

Pretender opened the door to leave and the sound of music reached me from somewhere in the distance, like it did every night. "What is that?"

"That's not for me to say," he said, turning back to me. "I'm sure Nero will tell you when he's ready."

"Are you? Because I'm not. That would require us to talk."

Pretender watched me from under the hood of his sweatshirt for several seconds, as though he wanted to say something, but then he shook his head, deciding to keep me in the dark like his master, and left, locking me in.

Restless, I paced the room, then with nothing else to do, I showered and got ready for bed.

As I pulled back the covers, my hands shook, but not from fear, from anger, from the helplessness I felt. No, I hadn't talked to Nero for the last three days, not since he forced me to feed, but that hadn't stopped him from coming to my room. He stood at the end of my bed for hours every night. I stayed still, quiet, like he demanded. I couldn't face another confrontation like the last, so I pretended I was asleep while that violet gaze burned through me.

How long could this go on? I wasn't sure I could take much more.

Desperate for any kind of escape, I selected a book from the shelf, one I'd read many times and flicked through the pages until I was sleepy.

Not long after I switched off the lamp, the sound of the lock turning reached through the darkness, followed by the flash of light from the hall as Nero opened and closed the door, shutting himself in with me. It never took long after I turned out the light. It was as if he stood outside my door, waiting for it.

My breath hitched, and my heart instantly beat faster. His

presence in this room felt heavy, and his rich scent filled the small space, making my skin hot and tight, making me crave things I didn't *want* to want from him.

And as the time ticked by, the longer I lay there while he did whatever it was he did, taking from me whatever it was he needed in this messed-up scenario, anger began to boil inside me.

No. I couldn't do this anymore, not for one more night. I couldn't, wouldn't cower under the covers another moment. I was hot, and irritated, and afraid, and furious, and with a hiss, I shoved back the covers and sat up.

Nero stood at the end of the bed. Utterly still. He wore dark pants and a white shirt, and his arms hung loose at his sides, the sleeves rolled up, revealing his tattooed forearms. He looked as cold as ever and as painfully beautiful as the first time I'd seen him.

He said nothing.

I held his gaze, not easy, but I managed it somehow. I wasn't sure what I was trying to do, give him a taste of his own medicine perhaps. Make him feel like the caged creature, or the featured attraction at the freak show, the way I did.

The silence was a living, breathing entity, like a third participant in this standoff between us.

His nostrils flared, and then his lips peeled back, revealing long, sharp fangs.

"How does it feel? Being treated like an animal at the zoo?" I said.

His head tilted to the side, then he licked his lips. "She speaks."

My belly went all weird. I got the feeling my refusal to speak the last few days had been getting to him.

He slid his hands into his pockets. "What did I say you were to do when I came into this room at night, Mina?"

"Honestly? I don't care anymore." I got out of bed and hoped he didn't see the way I trembled, though it wasn't like I could hide my fear, he felt it regardless. Still, I didn't want him to see me shake. "I may be your bonded, but we're not mated. I don't owe you respect, and you certainly haven't earned it. If you want something from me, then I expect to be paid in return."

One moment he was several yards away, the next he was looming over me. "And what is it you think you want, little doll?"

I bit my lip, dragging in a steadying breath as I gathered my courage. "I will give you anything you want, but in return I want my freedom. I want to be able to come and go from this room as I see fit, to go where I want, to live my life...and at night, I'll come back here, to this room, and I'll be your little doll. I'll lie in this bed, and you can stand at the end of it all goddamn night if that's what you want."

His lips curled up, but it wasn't a smile; it was a parody of one. Nero felt no amusement or joy. He wasn't capable of a sincere smile. "You think watching you sleep is payment enough for all you just asked for?" He ran the backs of his fingers down the side of my face, and I shivered from his cool touch. "Oh, no, bride, that wouldn't be nearly enough."

"Then name your price," I whispered.

His fingers curled around my jaw, and he tilted my head back. "There is no bargain, no offer you can make that will get you those things. Little dolls belong in their pretty little houses."

"Why are you doing this to me?"

His gaze dipped to my mouth. "Because I can."

We stared at each other in the darkness, his eyes almost glowing they were so bright. He hadn't fed in a while; they'd be darker if he'd fed. He hadn't fed since the garden when he'd had my blood.

His gaze slid to my mouth, and a low purr vibrated from him as he moved closer.

I froze, not sure what he was doing.

His nostrils flared and his chest expanded sharply as his fingers tightened on my jaw.

"Nero?"

He leaned in, coming closer, his lips...oh gods, they were about to make contact with mine—

I jerked my head to the side, and his mouth brushed my cheek instead. The purr morphed into a low growl. He kept hold of my jaw, then rested his forehead against the side of mine. "Are you trying to punish me, Lalka?"

"I told you I won't have you."

"You were begging for my fingers in your cunt three nights ago."

I flinched.

"Let me touch you," he said in a hushed voice that lifted goose bumps all over me. "You want to feel good again, Mina, I know you do."

I realized in that moment that I had power here. Yes, I was the one locked in this room, but we were blood bonded. My physical pain had stopped, his would only be getting worse with each passing day that he chose not to mate me.

Stepping back, I pulled from his hold. "No, *you* feel that way. You want me more than I will ever want you. How much pain are you in, Nero?"

He straightened but said nothing.

"When was the last time you fed?"

Still, he said nothing. He didn't need to. I knew the answers. He was suffering badly. "While you treat me like a prisoner, you will not get the privileges a bonded...a *mate* would get. You don't get to drink my blood or put your hands or your mouth on me." He was so much taller than me, but I straightened my spine, standing as tall as I could. "And you are not welcome in this bedroom at night. If you want to come in, you knock, and I'll decide if you're permitted to enter."

He blinked down at me several times.

I'd shocked him, but only for a moment.

I didn't see him coming. My feet left the floor, and a second later my back was to the wall, his large body pressed against mine.

"Put me down," I gasped.

He dipped his head, dragging his nose along my throat, then he nipped my skin, hard enough to break it. The scent of my blood reached me before he swiped his tongue over it sealing it again.

Lifting his head, he let me see the blood on his lower lip, my blood, then slowly licked it, telling me without words that not only could he take whatever he wanted from me, whenever he wanted to, and I had no way to stop him, but that he had the kind of control that I could only dream of.

I held his frigid stare. "Get out."

His nostrils flared again and he growled.

"Get out of my room," I said, fury and fear making my voice shake.

He released me suddenly, placing me back on my feet. They'd barely touched the ground, and he was gone.

A moment later, the sound of the lock being turned, echoed through the silent room.

Seven

NERO

I will give you anything you want, but in return I want my freedom.

Mina's husky voice filled my head, her words from two nights ago, and it wasn't the first time.

She'd demanded her freedom, but I couldn't give her that. She was asking too much.

If she refused me entry to her room, if being confined angered her enough to reject my touch, tonight I'd have to try something different.

Her refusal to let me close, to even speak to me, wasn't something I could tolerate. Truthfully, the more she denied me, the longer it went on, the closer I felt myself slipping to the edge of my sanity. Her pussy got wet when I was near, yet she would rather suffer than let me ease her need just to punish me. Her behavior was illogical. My bride confounded me, and infuriated me.

If I wanted to bend her to my will, I needed to be more strategic in my approach. I needed to throw Mina off-balance and regain control in a way that made her believe she still had some.

I never used the dining room in my apartment. I could eat human food; I just didn't need to. It had lost all appeal a long time ago, like all pleasures had. Maybe with Mina that might have changed as well? Tonight, I'd had Pretender go out and acquire a meal for Mina and me to share. Apparently, that's what females liked—to dine with their mates—and afterward, my hope was that her guard would lower enough that she would let me touch her.

I heard footsteps along the hall, and I turned to the door. From the article I'd read, surprises were enjoyed and welcomed as well.

The door opened and Pretender led Mina inside. She stopped sharply when she saw the table of food, then her gaze sliced to me.

"What is this?"

I gripped the back of the chair I stood behind. "I realized you'd not seen the rest of the apartment. I thought we could dine together, then I could give you a tour."

"Well, no, I haven't seen the apartment because I've been locked up like a prisoner since I got here," she said, but her voice was shaky.

I slid out the chair, choosing to ignore what she said. My newly awakening emotions were volatile, and anger that she wouldn't give me what I wanted was already rising inside me, and that wouldn't help at all. I was at least capable of seeing that. "I thought we could dine here this evening."

"No, thank you," she said. "I'd rather eat in my room alone."

A snarl tried to crawl up my throat, and I choked it down. I didn't like this feeling, not at all. How did she do this to me so easily? "Tonight you will eat in here, with me." I glanced at Pretender. "You can leave."

He gave me a nod and walked out, closing the door behind him.

"Come here, Mina."

"I don't want to."

"Now," I said, locking eyes with her.

Hers widened slightly, then she lifted her chin, showing me she wasn't happy, but finally made her way over to the seat I held for her. She sat and I took the chair closest at the head of the table.

"These dishes, they're your favorites, yes?"

She looked at the food laid out before her, and shrugged a delicate shoulder, making no move to reach for any of it.

"Pretender spoke to your mother's cook. She confirmed these were your favorite dishes."

"Well, she was wrong."

My lips peeled back and I sucked in a breath. "You won't eat it?"

She did the shoulder shrug again. "Beggars can't be choosers, I suppose," she said.

"No one has made you beg for food." I was barely resisting picking her up, setting her on the table in front of me, shoving up her dress, and feasting on her for my dinner instead.

"Prisoners don't get to choose, Nero. We don't get to choose anything."

"Tell me what your favorite meal is."

"Why do you care?"

I didn't know why, but for some reason, I did. Knowing what her favorite meal was had suddenly become incredibly important. "Tell me." She kept her lips pressed tight. "You said you don't get to choose; I'm letting you choose, Lalka."

She was silent several more seconds, then finally glanced my way. "I like pasta dishes and fresh baked bread and, for sweets, I like cake and anything with lemon in it."

I nodded. "I'll make sure you have some of your favorites from now on. If there's anything else you want to add to that list, just say so and I'll make sure you get it."

She made a little huffing sound and nodded, then she finally reached for the food in front of her, placing some roast meat and vegetables on her plate.

I did the same, hoping to make her feel at ease. I couldn't take another night like the last, banished from her room, desperate for her scent, her closeness.

We ate in silence, and though, yes, the food tasted good, was enjoyable even for the first time in centuries, I found her silence began to irritate me. I wanted to hear her speak. I wanted her eyes on me while she talked. I searched my mind for something to say to engage her in conversation. I was out of practice—I didn't know how to converse anymore—so coming up with a topic was difficult.

I searched the room for ideas, my gaze ultimately landing on a painting, a scenery.

"Do you enjoy art?"

She stilled. "Art? Like paintings?"

"Yes."

"I don't know. I suppose so. I've only ever looked at the ones in my parents' house and in books...you know, since I was kept at home after you went to the vampire court and announced your intention to claim me, to mate me, when I came of age. Which it turns out was a big fat lie. You don't actually want a mate though, do you? You just want a little doll?"

She was trying to get under my skin, to bait me, obviously, and she'd succeeded. I didn't like the way that made me feel either. "What about music?" I asked, attempting to change the subject.

"The music I listened to was restricted since my future mate would want his female innocent and untainted by the outside world," she said, not sparing me so much as a glance this time, then she slid a slice of tomato between her perfect rosebud lips.

I gripped the edge of the table. "I never asked for that."

She huffed a humorless laugh. "You had to know that's the way it would be, Nero. Did you think about what would happen to me at all when you stated your intention to claim me? Did you even spare me a thought? Did you wonder about my life and how it would change?"

No, I hadn't, not beyond her safety. "I wanted you safe."

"No, you wanted to make sure your possession was sparkly and new when you finally got to take it home. You turned me into a prisoner in my own home." She placed her knife and fork on the table. "And you've kept me that way...a prisoner."

The more we spoke, the more tumultuous my burgeoning emotions became and the farther away from my goal we got. "Would you like a tour of the apartment?" I needed to stop this line of conversation now, for both our sakes.

"Sure," she said, standing immediately and tossing her napkin on the table eagerly, too eagerly.

Placing my hand on the small of her back, I led her to the living room, pointing out the antiques and other items of value and possible interest to her, then directed her down the hall toward my bedroom.

Mina seemed to be searching for something as we walked, then after a few minutes, she visibly deflated. I realized what she was doing—she was looking for a way out, an escape.

I will find a way out of here. I will leave you, and I'll never come back.

As her vow filtered through my mind, a feeling like a storm swelled inside me. Didn't she know I would never let her leave? The knowledge that she was unhappy enough to want to run from me, that I was spectacularly failing at this, unable to make my young bride happy, had darkness, gnarled and ugly, spreading through me like poison.

I didn't know what the fuck to do. My reanimating emotions were growing inside me, but they were all jumbled and made me feel insane. I'd even reverted to asking August for assistance. He'd said his female didn't want to mate with him yet but liked to sleep in his arms. I couldn't remember the last time I'd allowed someone to sleep in my bed with me, but if that made Mina happy, I'd do it.

Would she even want to? Would I be able to hold her without touching her like I truly wanted to? Without this dark, twisted thing inside me taking hold and doing a lot more than wrap my arms around her?

All I knew was I wanted her to be happy here, happy with me.

I opened the door at the end of the hall and motioned her inside. She walked through, then stopped suddenly.

"Why am I in your bedroom?" She scanned the room, taking in everything, but her gaze kept darting back to the bed.

"Because this is where you will be sleeping tonight."

"No."

I bit back another snarl. "You wanted out of your bedroom, so this is where you will sleep instead."

"I told you that as long as you treat me like your prisoner, you don't get to be close to me in that way."

"I allowed you to leave your room. We dined together—"

"You think that's enough for me to let you...touch me? To do whatever it is you want to do to me?"

My control slipped. I hooked her around the side of the throat and pulled her to me and pressed my forehead to her temple, breathing her in. "Even now, I can smell how wet your cunt is, Lalka. All this denial, refusing me this way, is a waste of time. I know what you want, and you will give it to me."

She shoved at me, taking me off guard, and I stumbled back a step.

"Letting me leave my prison for a few hours, having a meal with me, that isn't freedom, Nero. This is just you trying to get your way without giving me anything at all. You know what I want, and this isn't it." She took a step back. "Take me back to my room. I'd rather be there alone than in here with you."

The roar erupted from me before I knew it was coming. "You will not deny me. Not anymore." I was having trouble naming the emotion battering me. My bones were molten beneath my flesh, burning under my skin. I wanted to tear at it, flay it from my body. I wanted to keep on roaring to release this jagged bolder in my chest as I dropped to the floor at her feet, curl my fingers around her legs and demand...*beg* her to let me have her. I told her I didn't want anything more from her, and I'd meant it, because I would break her if I took more, but right then, logic had left me.

I'd never wanted anyone the way I wanted Mina. No one denied me. Everyone I'd ever wanted, wanted me even more. That's what power got you. But this....this little female refused me over and over again. I'd been the one to decide not to mate her, and now it was all I could think about.

Mina had fucking *broken me*. She'd stripped me bare.

I felt like a fucking fool, something only my bride had ever accomplished, and that sent my rage higher. I stalked forward, and she backed up, hitting the wall. Curling my fingers around her slender throat, I leaned in. "You want me. Give in."

"Never," she bit out.

Her pulse fluttered wildly under my fingers, and the scent of her pussy intensified. "Give in to the hunger you're feeling. Are your juices coating your thighs, Lalka? I bet they are."

Her face flushed bright red. "You disgust me."

What was happening? Where was my control? My hands clenched and my vision blurred as everything inside me twisted into rage. I spun to the wall beside her and put my fist through it with another roar. When I turned back to Mina, her eyes were wide, her chest heaving.

I fucking hated that look in her eyes as well. Turning, I quickly stormed out of the room, locking her in, before I tore it down around us.

Somehow, I had to find a way to tame all the volatile emotions clashing inside me before I lost control completely.

Mina

I woke when the bedroom door opened and closed.

Somehow, I'd fallen asleep lying on his bed.

I'd fought it, but as the hours passed, exhaustion had won out.

Nero had returned.

My heart immediately sped up, and the blood in my veins and the flesh between my thighs heated, tingling in a way that was pleasurable. My body betrayed me every single time. But I would fight it for as long as I had to.

Gods, I felt his eyes burning into me from across the room. I wanted to tell him to leave, but this was his room not mine. Not that he would care how his presence made me feel. I hated that being this close to him made me feel almost as feral as he'd behaved before he'd walked out of this room several hours ago.

No, my bonded wouldn't care about my emotions, because he was utterly devoid of empathy.

A rustling sound came next. Was that the clink of his belt buckle?

I tried to keep my breathing even. Was he undressing?

The bed dipped, then Nero slid up behind me, his arm slipping around my waist.

"What are you doing?" I choked out, even as I ached for him to touch me. "I told you, I didn't want you to..." He nuzzled the back of my neck, breathing in my scent, and tingles danced across my skin. "Nero, I said n-no."

"I'm just going to hold you, Lalka. Nothing more," he said roughly.

I didn't know what to do, what to say. I didn't understand this game he was playing. I wanted to stick to my convictions, but it felt nice to be held. Too nice. "If you try to do anything else, I'll fight you," I said, even though I wasn't sure I meant it. I couldn't let him think he could control me. I had to make him understand how much I hated the way he was treating me.

I wanted to be his mate, not his prisoner.

At least I thought I wanted to be his mate. My feelings about this male were complicated and constantly changed.

"Okay, little doll," he said as he shuffled closer, so his entire body cradled mine. "You can have it your way...for tonight."

He lay motionless at my back, and the way he held me felt

maybe even a little awkward, as if this was unnatural for him. I supposed it was, but then what would I know?

Suddenly, I needed to know something, anything, that proved there was more to this cold, confusing male than what he'd shown me, or at the very least, that there once had been. Because I couldn't keep doing this, fighting for more, if there wasn't—if there never had been more. "Tell me something about before you were a member of The Five, before you lost your emotions."

He stilled even more, which seemed impossible, but somehow he had. "What do you want to know?"

"Do you remember your parents?"

"Only fractured moments of distant memories."

I couldn't imagine being so old, or so broken that I forgot my own parents. My stomach churned. "Did you have any brothers or sisters?"

There was a beat of deafening silence. "A sister. Dorotha."

"Do you remember much about her?"

"Yes."

"Is she still alive?"

"She was murdered by fae soldiers long ago."

The sudden need to comfort him surprised me. Still, I went with it and slid my hand over his that rested on my stomach. "I'm sorry, Nero." His voice hadn't changed, but he was affected, I could feel it. Anger literally radiated through his body to mine.

"It was a long time ago."

"But you loved her, didn't you?"

There was another pause, then his arm tightened around my waist slightly. "I suppose I did. It was her death that drove me to fight in the war, to become a member of The Five, so yes, I believe I loved her."

A kernel of hope ignited inside me. "When was the last time you held someone like this?" I asked, wanting to know more.

"I can't remember ever holding another like this."

"What about your sister? Did you ever hug her?"

"I'm...not sure. Possibly, when she was small. But I lost my emotions a very long time ago, Lalka. After that happened, I didn't require affection. I honestly can't remember ever feeling the need to hold anyone like this."

That sounded lonely to me. "But you do now? Feel the need, I mean?"

His fingers flexed against my belly. "I guess so."

"And do you....like it?"

Another beat of silence. "Yes," he said, finally smoothing my hair away from my throat and dragging his nose along my skin. "I think I do."

I didn't know what to say to that, and the silence stretched out.

"Good night, Mina," he said.

"Good night."

I was positive I'd never be able to fall asleep beside him, not after the way he'd lost control earlier, but I did. Somehow I drifted off almost immediately.

When I woke the next morning, Nero was gone, and Pretender was waiting to take me back to my room.

As soon as the other vampire shut me in my pink prison again, it was as if the madness of the night before had never happened, as if those quiet moments in the darkness in Nero's arms were all a dream.

Eight

NERO

"I NEED you to keep the club closed tonight," Constantine said.

I sat back in my chair, phone to my ear. "Why?"

He sighed. "My bonded is...lonely."

"And how will keeping my club closed cure that?"

"Our females, they've been alone, locked away from society since we claimed them, Nero. They need companionship. Rather than them seeking that from"—he growled low—"outside sources, I think that making friends with one another will at least be safe."

I gripped my phone tighter. Dining with her, taking her to my bed and holding her, answering her questions about my past, about Dorotha, whom I hadn't spoken about in longer than I could remember, hadn't worked. Maybe letting her spend time with my brothers' females would give her the sense of freedom she craved? I needed her where she was, where I knew she was safe from my enemies, but I couldn't fucking tolerate being barred from her room any longer. That separation from her only made the predator in me thirst for her even more violently.

I'd stood paralyzed outside her bedroom last night. I was a male who did whatever I wanted, whenever I wanted. Mina was mine, and if I wanted to go into her room, I could.

But I hadn't.

I hadn't done it because this turmoil inside me that she was responsible for was pushing me closer to the edge with each passing day, and sleeping beside her, in my bed, but still being denied all of her, had only made the wildfire inside me burn hotter.

I'd liked it, being that close to her.

She'd maintained steadfast in her resolve, though, while I'd burned for her.

I needed unrestricted access to her. I needed her compliant. That was the only way to stay in control.

What Constantine said made sense. Our females had been deprived of companionship for years, and for young females, I assumed that was difficult. A gathering like that would at least be safe, the club was secure, and we'd be there to make sure they were protected.

And maybe allowing her to meet with the other females, to form a friendship of some kind would please her and make her more biddable?

"Fine," I said to Constantine. "The Bank will stay closed tonight."

"I'll see you this evening, then," Constantine said and disconnected.

The upper-level club would be best. The Vault would need to remain open. I had customers that relied on it to feed. Thankfully, there were two entrances to The Vault, one in the upper level at the back of The Bank's main room that was manned at all times, and also an exterior door behind the main building.

"Have Monty redirect our clients to The Vault's back entrance tonight," I said to Pretender when he walked in. "The Bank will be closed."

My ward raised a brow but dipped his chin and left to do as I said.

I strode from my office and down the private stairs to the lower level. That heavy feeling in my chest grew with every step I took.

My skin felt tight, and I clenched and unclenched my fingers as my nerve endings felt as if they were sparking from the tips. The sensation wasn't pain. The pain was there, but this was something else, something even more threatening.

I had to be careful I didn't get lost to the sensations this female was causing in me.

You're already lost.

I ignored the voice in my head, refusing to believe it.

The reason I hadn't fucked her, hadn't mated her in that room when I finally got her to drink from me again, or when I held her in my bed the previous night, had finally become clear. It'd taken longer than it should to recognize, but now I could name the new feeling rapidly growing inside me and the weakness it had already caused.

Mina made me vulnerable in a way that was unacceptable. Dangerous.

Still, I couldn't stay away from her, and when I lifted my fist and knocked, I had to shake out my hand when I noticed how my fingers actually fucking trembled.

I heard her moving on the other side of the door, then she stopped and there was nothing but silence.

"Who is it?" she finally called.

She knew exactly who it was. She'd feel me this close the same way I did her, only she wouldn't feel the mind-numbing pain that came with it and the need to fuck like a rutting animal. "Nero."

More silence.

I waited for her to open the door, giving her what she asked for in the hopes that she would believe she had some power in this situation, and give in to my demands.

"You may enter," she finally said, this time closer to the door.

Unlocking it, I walked in. Mina was in another of her pink dresses. All were long, covering her body, but the way they hugged her breasts and waist was more than tempting enough.

"What do you want?" she asked, her spine straight, even as each exhale shook from the nervous energy I felt pouring off her.

There were things I needed from Mina, and I was beginning to realize that the only way to get them was to give her a sense of control. "I've thought about what you said, and I'd like to meet you halfway."

She looked surprised, then lifted her chin. "I'm listening."

"I am very old, Mina, and the nature of what I am means I stopped considering the feelings of others long ago. Why would I when I hadn't possessed them myself?"

I could tell her what I am, what I'd done, why I'd become the male I was, but I was trying to make this female trust me. Knowing that I was The Five's assassin, that the number of beings I'd killed in cold blood were in the thousands, that torture was a specialty of mine that I enjoyed very much, or the torture I'd suffered myself, would not help my cause.

She licked her lips, her eyes widening in anticipation.

"I have arranged a gathering tonight." An embellishment. It was all Constantine's idea, but taking credit could only help my cause. "My brothers are bringing their females to my club so you can...make friends."

"Friends." She drew in a sharp breath. "I can leave this room?"

"Yes."

Her entire face lit up, and somehow my beguiling bride looked even more stunning than she had before. "What kind of club? My mother attends a book club every Tuesday with her friends. Is it a book club?"

Her question took me aback. Her naivety made my chest ache for some reason. "No, in this instance it's a place where people come to dance and drink."

"And you have one?"

"I have two."

"And you'll show them to me?"

She was almost bouncing on the spot with excitement.

"One of them, yes."

"And will it be full of people?"

"I'm closing it, so it'll just be us—my brothers and their females."

Her smile didn't falter. "Thank you, Nero."

I inclined my head. "Be ready at nine," I said and left, because the urge to throw her on her bed, toss her long dress up, and fuck her into the mattress, then hold her like I had in my room, in my bed, was a creature all of its own. Being kept from her had fully awakened it, and that unguarded look of delight on her face, only teased it further.

Mina wasn't safe with me right then.

I needed to leave. I'd had my fix, measly as it was. I'd stood in the same room as her, breathed in her scent, heard her voice, and basked in her smile. That had to be enough. Any more right now was far too dangerous. So I turned and left before my control slipped completely.

Hopefully, after tonight, she'd stop fighting me, and let me back into her room. Only a small amount of time every day in her presence would help me regain and maintain that control.

If she didn't?

Gods help us both.

She was my drug and only a steady supply of my bride would stop me from snapping and glutting on her like the starved monster I was becoming.

~

Mina

My nerves skyrocketed when the knock at the door came, but it only took a split second to realize it wasn't Nero this time.

I strode over and opened the door.

Pretender stood there and his head jerked back the moment he laid eyes on me, then he laughed, the sound low and rough.

I looked down at myself, then back up. "Why are you laughing? Do I look stupid?" Pretender was a male of few words, but he'd never been unkind to me.

"Definitely don't look stupid, Mina. You look…really fucking good. Not sure Nero will be happy, though."

"Why?" Though I thought I knew the answer.

"You're showing a lot more skin than usual. If I'd known you'd use those scissors for this and not *arts and crafts*, I might not have brought them to you."

I chose the least offensive pink dress I had, then cut off the sleeves and taken up the length so it sat just above the knee. Pretender had shown me pictures on his phone earlier of the club when it was full of people. I'd been curious, and I'd been surprised when he had complied. What had stood out to me, though, was the way the females dressed. They weren't covered up like I'd always been made to. I didn't want to look silly in front of the other females, so I'd worked with what I had. "Might?"

He shrugged and chuckled again. "I kind of want to see Nero's reaction."

The male had a really nice laugh. "Where is he?"

"He's welcoming his guests and asked me to take you upstairs."

Pretender motioned to the door and took a step back, as always careful not to touch me in any way.

"This way," he said, leading me along the hall.

"What's through there?" I asked as we passed another door, one Nero hadn't opened the other night.

"Best you ask Nero that."

"Is that his other club?" It had to be. I could hear music, like the music I heard the nights Nero had come to my room.

Pretender glanced my way, well, I assumed he had. He always wore his hood pulled low, concealing most of his face and casting it in shadow. "He told you about The Vault?"

I nodded, kind of lying. He'd said there was another club, just nothing else. "Yes."

We went through a door at the end of the hall and up a steep staircase. At the top, we entered an office. It was Nero's. I knew because it smelled like him. There was a large desk and a huge window on one wall. It was mostly dark beyond it, but I could also see colored lights.

As soon as Pretender opened the door on the opposite side, the sound of music reached me, but it was different than the music I'd heard coming from the other door, the club Pretender called The Vault. Excitement filled me as we took another set of stairs, this time heading down.

I grabbed Pretender's sleeve, excited, and he jerked away like I'd struck him.

I quickly pulled my hand back. "Sorry."

"Fuck," he muttered and quickly yanked off his hooded sweatshirt, tossing it on the floor.

"What are you doing?" He looked up, and I gasped. He was... beautiful. Though that word didn't seem enough. I'd never seen a being that utterly beautiful in my life. So impossibly handsome that he didn't seem real.

He ignored my reaction to seeing his face properly for the first time. "If Nero scents you on me, he'll kill me."

He said it without fear but with utter certainty. "He wouldn't do that."

Pretender grinned and it was heart-stopping. "You're his bonded, Mina." That was all he said, as if that explained everything.

Then he opened the door and motioned me through. I stopped in my tracks when I saw Nero and his brothers across the room. "What if they don't like me?"

"They will."

"But what if they don't?" I didn't hear Pretender's reply because Nero had stopped talking to the massive vampires with him and had turned my way. I couldn't read his expression as that violet gaze sliced down my body to my bare legs and back up, lingering on my arms before coming to my mouth.

On shaky legs, my belly in knots, I started toward him. I'd almost reached him when his lips peeled back and he flashed his fangs. My step faltered.

Was he angry?

He strode forward, his fingers curling around my wrist. "What are you wearing, Lalka?"

I blinked up at him. "What do you mean?"

"You have taken a pair of scissors to your dress."

"I know."

He bared his teeth again. "If we weren't in this room with males I trust, I would drag you back to your room, put you over my knee, and spank you before I made you change into something else."

Anger flashed through me, taking me by surprise. "You are not my father, Nero. You are my mate, or you're supposed to be. I am a grown female, not a child to be punished. What I wear is my choice despite your attempts to control that as well. Get used to seeing me like this because I will not dress like a child...or a...*a doll* any longer, and if that means chopping up every gown in my closet, I will."

He leaned in, his mouth brushing my ear. "No one has ever gotten away with speaking to me the way you do, Mina, and I've decided, that neither will you."

I tilted my head back. "What are you going to do?"

His gaze moved over mine and he grinned, one of his emotionless grins—no, not totally emotionless this time because his eyes shone bright.

"Mina!" A chorus of voices reached me over the music.

I turned and four females, the same females I'd seen briefly at the blood moon ceremony, stood across the room and were waving me over. I spun back to Nero.

His nostrils flared, and I knew he was scenting me. "Go meet your new friends," he said, then released me.

Fighting back the nerves, I strode over to them. I was scared, shy, but I would not waste this opportunity.

They instantly surrounded me.

"I've been so desperate to meet you," one of them said. "Are you okay? Is Nero being kind to you?"

This female, whoever she was, was the first person to ask me that since the ceremony, and without my say-so, tears filled my eyes.

They gathered around me more tightly, comforting me without question, offering kindness. I hadn't realized the toll this whole thing had taken on me until this moment. I'd been in survival mode since I got here, and it felt like this was the first breath I'd taken.

Another female took my hand and they kept me hidden, forming a shield as they ushered me over to a booth on the other side of the club.

"Talk to us," another of them said.

"Whatever you're going through, we'll understand," a small female with soft features and vibrant lilac eyes said.

I didn't even know their names, but I felt a kinship with them instantly and blurted it all out. About the bedroom that was a replica of the one I'd had in my parents' home, about the pink dresses and the midnight visits and tricking me into feeding from him by using my own instincts against me, then thinking he could win me over with a meal out of my room. When I was finished, none of them seemed remotely shocked.

A female with fiery red hair and a dusting of freckles took my hand. "I know this whole thing is...weird and confusing. I know they're"—she tilted her head toward our bonded males—"weird and confusing, but they're not like other males, and even if we hadn't been locked in our houses for years and shut off from the

72

world, this would still be just as hard." She smiled kindly. "I'm Lucinda, by the way. That's Effie, Delphine, and Ana."

Ana smiled as well. "They're warriors and incredibly old and have very little in the way of emotion, if any. I'm not giving them a pass for the way they're behaving, but as terrifying as they seem, or had seemed to us, I get the feeling we're just as terrifying to them."

"Once you mate, they don't seem so terrifying anymore," Lucinda said, her cheeks pink.

"You're mated?"

She nodded. "Last night."

"How was it?" Effie asked, eyes wide.

She chewed her lip, then grinned. "Really, really good. Amazing, actually. I don't know...things feel different between us now. I know it's scary, and I know you want to strangle them...or bash them over the head with something, but I promise it gets better."

A laugh burst from me. "I would have stabbed Nero if I'd had the chance."

Ana nodded. "They're so intense, and the arrogance is unmatched." Her expression changed. "Ana," she said in a low voice, while she narrowed her eyes and lifted her chin, in imitation of her bonded's voice, "if you don't stop flouncing around in front of me in those fucking shorts, I'll fucking burn them." Her voice was mocking and deep, then she pulled a face, one that I assumed was supposed to be intimidating and arrogant.

We all burst out laughing.

The males turned our way, their eyes narrowed in the same way Ana's had just done, and everyone laughed again, harder.

The music changed, and Delphine grabbed on to my and Effie's hands. "Should we dance?"

Lucinda nodded. "I think we should. Who knows when we'll get this chance again?"

We laughed, giddy as we ran out to the dance floor. None of us knew what we were doing. The only dancing we'd done was in the privacy of our rooms, and some of us probably not even then, but that didn't matter. For the first time in five years, I felt free.

Maybe it was only an illusion, and it would all end when the night did.

But I planned to make the most of every minute.

Nine

MINA

My feet hurt, but I couldn't stop smiling.

Lucinda grabbed my hand, and I watched as she made eye contact with Rainer, then blushed and smiled.

"You're lucky. Rainer must be a kind male."

She snorted. "He was anything but kind when I first went home with him. He was surly and snappy and distant." Then she shook her head and her face softened. "But he was pushing me away because he was afraid he'd hurt me."

"Really?" I glanced up at Nero, and my heart thumped when I found his gaze locked on me. I quickly turned back to Lucinda.

"There's more to these males than they choose to show us and, I guess, more than even they know. I had to force Rainer's hand. I was scared, but I refuse to live an eternity miserable. My parents love each other deeply. I've seen what that looks like, and I wanted it, so I made it happen."

"How?"

She bit her lip and blushed a deeper pink. "Their drive to mate us is extremely strong and painful." I knew that part, about the pain, though Nero hid it well. "So, I used my, uh...body to...to tempt him."

"You did?" Heat flushed through me.

She nodded and giggled. "I pretended I didn't know I was doing it. He fought hard, trying to hold on to his control, but they were no match for me."

"They?"

She snapped her mouth closed.

"Lucinda?"

Her gaze darted to her mate, and she bit her lip, then looked back at me. "Rainer has an...inner beast, and sometimes he transforms completely. That's why he was so scared that he might hurt me." She squeezed my hand. "Rainer's beast may be unique among his brothers, but I think they all have their own inner beasts in one form or another. It's our job to tame them, and to take what we deserve." She straightened her spine. "They claimed us, but no one said we don't get to claim them as well."

I stared down at her, my pulse racing. My parents loved each other as well; it was something I'd always wanted for myself. Was Nero's behavior and his odd demands because he was scared he'd hurt me, like Rainer had been with Lucinda? Sometimes I looked into his eyes, and what I saw staring back froze the blood in my veins. He was struggling for control, even I could see that.

What would happen if I fought for more? If I pushed and tempted Nero?

What would happen if I made him lose control completely?

Nero

"Did you have fun?" I asked Mina as we headed down the stairs, heading back to her room. I needed to know. She'd seemed to be enjoying herself tonight, but I needed to hear her say it for some reason.

She smiled up at me. "It was the best night of my entire life."

I will give you anything you want, but in return I want my freedom.

Her words reverberated in my head, coming back to me time and again since she'd said them. After finding out that Rainer, of all our brothers, had mated his female, I was struggling to hold on to my resolve. Not to mention seeing her dancing in that pink dress that she'd taken a pair of scissors to, and baring too much of her smooth, supple skin.

It also didn't help that I needed to feed. I had to get away from her, now, before it was too late, before I snapped and took her vein, then proceeded to take everything else I wanted from her.

Pretender was walking toward us. "Take Mina to her room."

She spun toward me, a look in her eyes that made my stomach grip impossibly tight. "You're leaving?"

"There's something I need to do."

"But—"

Somehow, I turned away, cutting her off. I forced myself to walk back down the hall, then quickly used my key and strode through my private entrance into The Vault.

The club was busy, as always, and I stood there, scanning the room for a donor. I wanted Mina's blood, but drinking from her alone would only make my craving for her even worse. I hadn't fed since the blood moon ceremony, and usually that wouldn't be a problem. I could go weeks without feeding, but not with my little bonded so close.

I took my place in the booth at the back of the club. It was in shadow, and a good place to watch what was going on. A male, a regular here, and one I'd never fed from, walked by. He'd do. I crooked my finger at him.

The male froze for a split second, then rushed to my side.

Feeding was a sexual experience, and in the past, I would have allowed this male to get himself off while I fed. Once upon a time, I might have fucked him. But fucking anyone but Mina didn't interest me—as it was, I'd have to choke this male's blood down.

"Sir, I am at your serv—"

"Did I say you could speak?"

He quickly shut his mouth.

I dispassionately took in the pulsing vein at his throat. I desperately needed to feed, but my fangs wouldn't even drop for him. That had never happened to me before, and now I knew they wouldn't, not for him and not for anyone else because they weren't my bonded, they weren't Mina. She was all I wanted.

With a snarl, I shoved him away. "Leave."

He scrambled back, almost tripping in his haste to escape. Pretender appeared at my side a moment later, placing a glass of bourbon on the table in front of me.

"Did she say anything when you took her to her room?" I asked him.

"No, she was quiet."

Every muscle in my body tensed in anticipation of me standing, of walking back through this club, back into the hall, and down to her room.

Why was I resisting? I could keep her safe. I was one of the most feared vampires in this realm—and in many others.

Because she makes you weak.

Growling under my breath, I snatched up my glass and downed its contents, but it wasn't what I fucking wanted.

A familiar heartbeat reached out to me suddenly, beating fast, frantic, and my head shot up in time to see Mina enter the club on the other side of the room.

"How did she get out of her room?" I snapped at Pretender.

The younger vampire quickly searched his pockets. "My keys, they're gone. She fell...she grabbed for me, she—"

"Are you saying she picked your pocket?" I scented him. "Then why can't I smell her on you?"

"Because I changed."

"Wise." The mood I was in, I would have torn him to fucking shreds if I'd scented her on my ward. There is no way he would have given her his keys willingly. He would never betray me that way. It didn't matter that he'd been a loyal servant to me for many years, with my lack of control, there would have been no stopping it, and he knew it.

"I'll take her back to her room," he said.

I shook my head, stopping him before he took a step. "Leave her, but stay close, make sure no one touches her."

Pretender nodded and slipped around the edge of the room.

Sitting back, I watched her take in the club. Her pulse was wild, and over the scent of lust and blood, hers reached out to me, coiling around me tight.

My little doll thought she'd outwitted me, but I realized as she stood there, blushing and wide-eyed, that what she was seeing in this room was having an effect on her. Her control was nowhere near as strong as mine, and maybe seeing others drink and fuck would make her hunger for my vein. Maybe it would have her begging for my touch. I wanted that on a primal level, for my female to want me, to need that from me, with a ferocity that consumed me.

She still hadn't seen me, but I could tell she was searching for me. As she got closer to where I was sitting, I stood and slipped into the shadows, moving around the edge of the room so I was standing behind her.

So many eyes were on her now, so many lustful, hungry eyes.

No, that wouldn't do at all.

Closing the space between us, I grabbed her slender throat from behind and pressed my mouth to her ear. "Not enough fun for one night, Lalka?"

She sucked in a startled breath but didn't try to pull away. "I— I was looking for you."

"Were you? And why is that?"

She was panting now. "Because I wanted to spend some time with you."

I didn't know what game she was playing, but if she wanted to play, I'd play. I curled my other arm around her waist and walked her forward, to the back of the club, where my booth was in shadows.

Sitting, I pulled her onto my lap, so her back was pressed to my front. I expected her to try to wriggle away, to fight me, to tell me I wasn't permitted to touch her, but she didn't. She sat where I put her, posture rigid.

I gently took hold of her jaw. "You went to all this trouble to escape your room and get into my club because you wanted to spend time with me, yes? Because you wanted to see what was going on in this room? Well, I'm in a giving mood, Mina." I pulled her more firmly against me and pressed my mouth to her ear. "So you'll sit here, and you will watch."

Ten

MINA

I fought not to squirm.

The scent of blood was making me crazy, and I couldn't look away from all that was happening in the room around me.

"What is this place?"

"A feeding club. This is where blood drinkers and donors meet and make mutually beneficial transactions."

His voice slid over me, low and smooth, and I couldn't stop my shiver. "Donors?"

"People, others who like to be bitten and fed from." His warm breath teased my skin. "They get sexual gratification from it. The blood drinkers get what they need and so do the donors."

I didn't like the thought of Nero doing that, of him feeding from someone else, of him...touching them. "Have you done that? Have you made a mutually beneficial transaction with the donors who come here?"

"Yes," he said. "Many times."

No. I didn't like that at all. In fact, the idea of it was so abhorrent, I found myself pushing back against him, the action involuntary, as if to shield him from anyone in this room who might think they could offer themselves to him. It made no sense. I didn't like this male. Until tonight, when he'd finally let me out of my room for a few hours, he's been nothing but cold, cruel, and manipulative.

But that was the power of fate, of a bond like ours. Still, I found I wanted to hurt him back, because the thought of him being with another did hurt. It was stupid, of course he had. He was old. He would have fed from many others over the centuries, but that didn't seem to make any difference.

"Maybe I should choose a donor to feed from," I said.

His fingers were back at my throat in an instant, his fang grazing my ear. "If you feed from anyone but me, little doll, I will skin them, shred them in front of you until there is nothing left but gore. Do you understand?"

His words should scare me. Instead, they made my heart race faster and the deep throb between my thighs grow heavier. "Does that mean you'll only drink from me?" I whispered.

He nipped my ear, and I shivered again. "Is that what you want?"

It was. I was already at a disadvantage with this male. I didn't want to give him anything else to hold over me, but then I thought about what Lucinda said and I decided if I wanted to claim my mate, to break through the ice and thaw the emotions that were buried deep, I needed to tame Nero's inner beast, whatever it was. I needed to disarm him, and giving him the truth would hopefully do that.

"Yes... I want you to only drink from me," I confessed.

"Then no more drinking from a glass, Lalka. No more barring me from your room, and you can have what you want." He sucked my earlobe gently. "I gave you freedom tonight, Mina, does that mean I get everything?"

"Not everything," I forced myself to say. "That was only a taste of freedom, and I'll need a lot more than that before I fully surrender to you." Lucinda had pushed Rainer to his breaking point, and if I wanted Nero to give me everything, then I would have to do the same.

He purred low and rough. "So does that mean I get a taste of you, little doll? It's only fair, a taste for a taste."

His cool lips and warm breath caused goose bumps to lift across my skin. The scent of blood and the moans of pleasure filling the room had my head spinning. My body was tight and hot and hungry for more than just blood. I was supposed to entice him, instead he'd turned the tables on me. "Yes," I said, giving him the truth again and hoping he didn't make me regret it.

"I can smell how wet your cunt is. Does it ache?"

A whimper slipped free. "Yes."

"Would you like me to ease it?"

I rubbed my thighs together, squeezing them tight, but it didn't help. Only Nero could make it go away. "Yes...please."

"Say that again, little doll."

He wanted me to beg for him to make me feel good. If I hadn't been in this room, if I didn't feel so out of control, I would have refused, but I needed relief. I needed him to touch me so badly I shook. "Please," I whimpered. "Please, Nero."

A long, drawn-out rumbling sound vibrated from his chest, startling me. I expected him to lift me to my feet, to lead me from the club, but instead he turned me on his lap so my side was pressed to his front, my bottom cradled by his muscled thighs.

His hand slid up under my dress, and I slammed my knees together. "What are you doing?"

"What you asked for, bride."

"But everyone will see."

"Look around you, Mina, no one gives a fuck what we're doing. They're taking their own pleasure. Besides, if anyone looks at you while I'm pleasuring you, I'll kill them, so it won't matter."

I blinked up at him. "You'd kill them?"

His hand traveled down the back of my thighs, then easily slid up between them. A gasp left me when his fingers brushed where I wanted him to touch me so badly.

"Unclench your thighs," he ordered softly.

I did, feeling hot and desperate and weak. It was wrong, but Nero's threat to anyone who looked at us made my belly swirl in a pleasant way. He didn't want anyone to look at me like this either. Honestly, that made me feel safe here in his arms.

"Very good," he said. "My little Lalka is drenched. Panties so fucking soaked they're ruined." The sound of tearing fabric came next. He tore my underwear from me, then tucked them in his pocket. "The scent of your need is so heavy, bride, that everyone in this room can smell it. Look," he said against my ear as he slid his thumb along the seam of my slick flesh. "Look around you. They're wild. You caused this, Mina, you did this."

He was teasing me. My scent was only one of many in this room, but as I looked around, I squirmed against his hand, seeking more, needing more. The beings in this room were moving against each other, doing things I couldn't name, things I didn't understand, but the pleasure they were feeling was blatant to see.

Nero kept up that slow, steady slide of his thumb, teasing me, not giving me more, not until he was ready. I clung to his shirt, caught between wanting more and reveling in his wonderful torment.

I watched as a female moved on top of a large vampire on one of the couches. The male was drinking from her bare breast, while she writhed, moving up and down, sometimes bouncing, sometimes staying tight to him and swiveling her hips. She threw her head back and cried out. At the sound of her pleasure, my thighs squeezed around Nero's wrist. I was panting now. The vampire dragged his tongue over his puncture marks and lifted the limp female off him, propping her up on the couch beside him.

I gasped. "What is that?"

"What?" Nero asked roughly.

"Sticking up from his...his hips." It was long and thick and glistening.

The big vampire crooked his finger, and another female walked up, straddled his hips, then reached down, took the flesh in her hand, held it between her thighs, and sat. The glistening length disappeared inside her, then the vampire bit her and she threw her head back with a cry of pleasure as well.

Nero had gone silent beneath me.

"What was that, Nero?" I asked again, my heart beating wildly as I watched the second female bounce and grind on top of the vampire while he drank from her throat.

"Males and females are made differently, Mina, you have to know that?" he finally said.

My face heated. "Well, yes, I just didn't know how... I've never seen..."

He took my jaw in his hand and turned my face toward him, his eyes locked with mine. "That, Lalka, is a cock."

I blinked up at him. "Oh." I had no idea what that meant.

"Cocks are soft usually, but they get hard, growing thicker, longer, when a male is around someone they want to fuck. And little dolls have an opening that is made especially for it." His thumb slid lower, rubbing over a part of me that often felt empty when I was near this male. I'd touched it, ran the tip of my finger over it, but I'd been too afraid to do more than that. "It feels tight and wet and hot when we slide inside." He pushed his thumb inside me, and I moaned at the intrusion. He dragged it back out, then slid back in, and my thighs spread wider all on their own.

I gripped his shirt tighter, then he slid his thumb out and instead filled me with one long, thick finger. My nails were close to tearing the fabric of his shirt as I gasped and whimpered.

"Feels good, doesn't it, bride?"

I bit my lip hard to stop the needy sounds coming from me, and I tasted my own blood.

That's when I realized what the hard thing underneath me

was. Nero's cock was hard. It was long and thick and straining against his trousers beneath me. "Do you want to put your...your cock inside me, Nero?"

"Yes," he said roughly, his gaze dipping to the blood on my lip. "I want to contort your tight little body in all sorts of ways while I fuck you senseless, Mina. You have no idea how badly."

His fingers moved faster, sliding deeper, and I fisted his shirt at his throat to hang on and pressed my flushed face to his cool skin. I felt it building, the thing that Nero had done to me several times now, but this time it was more intense, more out of control. *I* felt out of control. "Then do it." I moaned against his tattooed throat. "I feel so empty. Oh gods...please, Nero. I need it."

He growled and added another finger. "I would destroy your little cunt, Mina, the way I want it right now. I'd make it hurt. You're not ready for the way I'd fuck you."

My hips were mindlessly rocking against his hand as he filled me with his fingers, thrusting into me over and over again. It was too much, I was too full, yet it wasn't enough. I wanted him. I wanted his cock. "I don't care if it hurts. I want it to hurt." My fangs had extended, and they grazed his throat. "I need... I have to—"

"Bite," he snarled. "Now."

I struck, sinking my fangs into his throat, and as soon as his blood hit my tongue, I broke, shattering around his fingers. I pulled my fangs from his flesh so I could cry out and warm blood slid down my chin.

When I opened my eyes, blood had dripped on the bodice of my dress. Panting, I quickly sealed my bite, then dragged my hand across my chin, staining my skin with more.

My gaze shot up to Nero, and he was watching me with starved eyes. I was instantly caught in his predator's gaze.

"Messy, little doll," he said, lifting his fingers. He held them up so I could see that they still glistened from being inside me...then Nero slid them into his mouth and sucked them clean. He took my jaw in his hand next and swiped his tongue up my chin, lapping up the blood before sucking on my lips.

It felt amazing. Then he swept his tongue into my mouth, and my head spun, my body reigniting from his kiss.

His blood and my juices mingled between us. I wanted his hand between my thighs again. I ached for it. I was like some wanton creature when he touched me this way, when he fed me.

"Now it's my turn," he said, and a chill slid down my spine.

"Your turn?" I asked breathlessly.

"To feed."

My pulse sped up, but I wanted it, badly. I tilted my head to the side, exposing my throat without even a second thought. He could have me. "Take it."

He dipped his head, his lips drifting over my sensitive skin, but he didn't bite. Instead, his mouth went to my ear. "You're just going to give in so easily, Lalka? After the way you've teased and tormented me?" He made a tutting sound. "I don't think so."

I turned back to him. "I don't understand—"

"Run," he said, eyes flashing with excitement. "I'll give you a head start, but if you want your freedom, then you need to fight for it."

"Wha—"

"Run."

My heart slammed into the back of my ribs. He was serious. If I wanted any kind of freedom, I'd have to play by his rules. I'd have to play his games, because that's what this was to him. A game.

I clumsily got off his lap, stumbling back, unsteady after feeding, after Nero touching me in front of a room full of people. He sat unmoving, watching me as I backed up a shaky step.

I licked my lips, and his nostrils flared, then he jerked forward. I shrieked and spun away.

Racing through the main room, I stumbled over my own feet as I headed for the privacy screen in front of the side entrance I'd come through earlier. Shooting a glance over my shoulder, I saw Nero stand, buttoning his jacket as he stepped around the table.

Oh gods.

Rounding the screen, I grabbed the handle and yanked the door open. I exploded into the hall, and not knowing where else to go, kicked off my shoes and ran toward the door that led to his office and the empty club beyond it, where I'd been earlier. I tried to tread as soundlessly as I could as I sprinted up the stairs and into Nero's office.

Racing through it, I opened the door on the other side, descended the stairs, and burst out into the now dark and empty club. It felt different without the lights or the music. Cold, eerie.

My sight was okay in the dark, but nothing like Nero's would be. A vampire his age would have no trouble seeing in utter darkness.

Music suddenly blared through the speakers, and I screamed, stumbling back, desperately searching for an escape. The exit was across the dance floor, on the other side of the room, and I sprinted for it while the pounding beat vibrated through my chest and made it impossible to hear, to think clearly.

I reached the main door that led out onto the street and fumbled with the locks, yanking on it, but there was no getting out that way.

Lights started, flashing between bright and dark so fast it distorted the room around me. I panted, my pulse racing so fast I was dizzy.

Groping for the wall, I used it to ground myself. I needed to go back. I needed to get to my room. I was safe in my room.

Something tugged hard at my dress. Nero. I spun around, my arms out. Cool air hit my skin as the fabric was torn open at my back. I screamed, searching, flailing, but he was too fast. Again and again, he rushed past, tearing, pulling, ripping my dress until I stood there in only a bra since my shredded panties were already in his pocket.

I pressed against the wall, tears streaming down my face, shaking, confused, overwhelmed...and wetter than I'd ever been before. Aching more deeply than I ever had. I wanted this to end, for him to stop, yet desperate for him to strike.

Trying to cover myself, I frantically searched the room—

Suddenly, he was in front of me, his fingers tight around my throat. His lips curled up in that imitation of a smile that sent ice through my veins. A moment later, his hand slid up, taking my jaw, and he jerked my head to the side—then he struck.

I screamed—and my inner muscles clamped down, clutching wildly, repeatedly at nothing while his big body pinned my smaller naked one to the wall. His cool lips pressed against my skin while his hot tongue worked my vein, massaging it so I'd bleed faster for him. It felt so incredibly good, and tension swirled low in my belly a second time.

I gripped his arms as he sealed his bite, then he lifted me higher, sliding me up the wall and pinning me there with his body. Yanking down the cups of my bra, he sucked my breast into his mouth, forcing a groan out of me before he struck again, sinking his fangs deep into my flesh, like the female I'd seen tonight. I arched against the wall and came again, flailing, crying out as he sucked and teased and fed.

He hadn't even touched between my legs, but my thighs were slick, my desire sliding down them. I'd feel shame if it was possible to feel anything other than soul-shattering pleasure.

Sealing that bite as well, he pulled me off the wall. Next thing I knew, I was on a table, and he was sucking and licking my inner thigh. My head spun and I struggled to catch my breath—then his mouth was *there*, his hands holding me wide, licking and sucking the most private part of me.

And it was—wonderful.

Oh gods, I wanted more.

As if he could read my mind, he thrust two fingers inside me and slid his tongue higher, teasing a spot that had me reaching down to fist his hair and lifting my hips for more—

He struck again.

I shrieked, bowing against the table, and came a third time, but this time I felt a gush of something that wasn't blood as I trembled and cried out, my body convulsing against the cool wooden surface.

Nero slowed, lapping at me more gently, savoring, and I whimpered, moaning helplessly as little shocks of pleasure pulsed through my body.

He finally straightened, and a moment later, I was dragged down the table so my spread legs were on either side of his hips. The flashing lights made this whole thing feel surreal, a dream. I watched as Nero, his image fragmented by the rapidly pulsing lights, yanked open the front of his trousers, wrapped his fist around his long, thick cock, and stroked so fast he was a blur. I couldn't take my eyes off him. Then he grabbed one of my thighs, shoved it up and out, and angled his cock down.

I braced, expecting him to push it inside me. Instead something hot splashed over my swollen, needy flesh. Nero was focused between my thighs, and when he released his hard length, he rubbed his fingers in the liquid before shoving them back inside me. He leaned over me, his eyes locked on mine as he thrust his fingers deep and hard and fast.

He said nothing, and neither did I. I stared back, panting, as he brought me swiftly back to the edge of insanity. He didn't bite me this time, though, no, he watched as I lost control all over again, gripping fiercely at his pumping fingers and calling out his name.

Finally, I collapsed back, panting, unable to move as he slid his fingers from me, and I watched as he did up his pants, then removed his shirt, revealing his muscled and tattooed chest for the first time. Sitting me up, like the doll he called me, he put my arms through the shirt sleeves and buttoned it up.

He lifted me then, carrying me through the empty club and up the stairs to his office. He hit a button, and the music and lights stopped. Then he carried me back along his private hall, down the stairs on the other side, and to my room.

Laying me on the bed, he tossed the covers over me. He was going to leave. He was going to leave me locked in here again.

"Don't," I choked out. "Don't leave me in here by myself."

He looked down at me dispassionately, swiping his thumb over my cheek. "It's for your own good, Lalka." Then he turned and walked out.

I picked up the book beside my bed and flung it at the door with a scream of rage.

This wasn't over. He may think he'd won, but he hadn't.

If he wanted to play games, fine.

But they had only just begun.

Eleven

NERO

I'D ONLY WANTED to tempt her last night, to make her lose her head and drink from me.

Instead, I'd snapped, my control slipping beyond my ability to regain it. That never happened, not since I was young, not since I was that wild thing, but after she'd buried her little fangs in me, the monster had taken over because it hadn't been enough.

Fear and desire were an intoxicating mix.

Making chase, hunting my prey made me so fucking hard.

I'd expected her fear. I knew chasing her would terrify her. I'd counted on it. I thought I could use it to stop myself when I caught her.

But she'd fucking loved it.

My little doll had gotten so wet, her juices were sliding down her supple thighs. Being chased, the fear and anticipation of being caught, had excited her. Stopping was the last thing I wanted to do when that realization had sunk in.

My innocent Mina had gotten off on the chase—on the fear—as much as I had.

The fates knew what they were doing when they chose my bride, and that realization had been tormenting me all night.

I couldn't remember the last time I felt that way—that I'd felt anything.

Day by day, she was chipping away at my defenses, shattering my resolve—weakening me. Even now, all I could think about was the taste of her blood and her cunt. All I could hear were the sounds of her screams and her calling my name when she came for me.

With the way she affected me, I knew using my mouth, my fingers to pleasure her wouldn't be enough for long. I'd barely stopped myself from fucking her on that table last night, mating her in truth. Soon, I'd need more, and though my needs and wants had been few the last couple of centuries, I wasn't used to denying myself.

Resting my hands on the frame of her door, I gritted my teeth as the urge to go inside slammed into me. I had a meeting tonight. The war between the fae and the vampires had ended when the new king had taken the throne, but there were members of the previous royal house who were out for revenge.

My services were still very much needed.

"Nero?" Mina's voice came through the door.

I stayed silent.

"I can smell you," she said, surprising me. "I can also see your shadow under the door."

"What do you want, Mina?" My throat felt impossibly tight. I hadn't thirsted for blood like this since I was young, but now not anyone's blood would do, only hers.

"I need your help...please."

Just hearing her say please had me hardening against the front of my trousers. My self-restraint right then, with her taste still on my tongue, was nonexistent. I should walk away and come back when I'd mastered the unrelenting need still stirring inside me, but I couldn't do it.

Instead, I unlocked the door and pushed it open.

Mina stood by her bed in only a pair of pink lace panties and matching bra, her eyes were wide, her hands trembling slightly at her sides. With a snarl, I slammed the door shut after me in case Pretender walked by and saw her like that.

I rounded the bed. "What do you think you're doing? Put your clothes on, now."

She looked up at me, one of her little fangs, biting down on her lower lip. Just the sight of her fangs had my gut clenching and my mouth going dry.

"That's why I called you in. Pretender said you were going out tonight, and I wasn't sure what to wear." She motioned to the bed, where two dresses were laid out, both of which had been given the same treatment as the one she wore last night.

"You aren't going anywhere," I said.

"Yes, I am," she answered and, straightening her shoulders, stepped closer. "I have the key to that door hidden somewhere in this room. Either you take me with you or I walk out of here in my underwear the moment you leave, let myself into The Vault, and bury my fangs in the first handsome donor who offers me his vein."

Irrational rage slammed into me. I hadn't felt anger in centuries, but it had been returning again and again since I'd brought Mina here. "I've already told you, if you feed from anyone else, I'll kill them. Are you willing to risk another's life, just so you can prove a point?"

She held my gaze. "Yes, I am. You can kill every donor in your club if that's what it takes, but I don't think that would be very good for your business. I don't think anyone would want to offer to feed your customers if they're worried the great Nero Kossek, feared member of The Five, might murder them."

She was far too fucking clever. "I don't take kindly to threats, Mina."

"And I don't take kindly to being a prisoner. So choose a dress...or I will."

Her heart was pounding. Despite the bravado, she was definitely afraid. This little stand she was making had taken all of her courage. "I have a meeting; this isn't some social event."

"I don't care. I'm going with you," she said.

I should say no. Agreeing to this would only make her think she was the one who held the power in this situation, and she very much did not. But I found that I wanted to reward her for her bravery, and that I...I liked the idea of having her with me. Pretender could watch her while I was in my meeting.

This display of bravery definitely deserved an appropriate response. Reward, yes. Courage should always be acknowledged. But my little Lalka also needed to be punished for her defiance, and I knew exactly what that punishment should be.

I was playing with fire, I knew that. But the cracks had already formed, my emotions were slowly seeping to the surface, and there was no repairing those fractures now or turning back time. It was too late for that.

Mina was mine. Perhaps I should just enjoy her any way I saw fit.

"Very well."

Her face lit up. "You'll take me with you?"

"Yes," I said, spotting a bag on the bedside table, something gold poking from the top catching the light. Her jewelry, I guessed, and judging by how rounded the bag was, all of it stuffed into that small bag. The only items she had of value.

"Well? Which dress do you like best?" she asked.

I eyed the dresses she'd laid out and lifted a deep pink lace one, the color of the peonies that had filled the flower boxes outside Mina's bedroom window. The gown had been cut short, but the sleeves had been left long. I'd be able to see peeks of her skin through the lace. "This one."

I held it out, and she curled her fingers around it. Instead of releasing the fabric, I tugged her forward. She stumbled closer, and I slid my fingers into her long blond hair, tilting her head back. Her breath rushed from between her luscious, cherry-colored lips.

"You know there will be a price to pay for this, don't you, little doll?" But not just for her defiance—for her plan to try to escape me tonight. Why else would she have removed her jewelry from its box on her dresser? Why else would she have every piece stuffed into that little bag. If she brought it with her tonight, I'd know I was right.

Her tongue darted out, sliding across her lower lip, and my abdominal muscles tightened. "Yes," she whispered.

Her eyes were wide, but they glittered with anticipation. Did she really think she could escape me? That I'd ever let her leave?

I took in her lovely body. Oh, yes, I'd enjoy tearing those flimsy scraps of lace from her later when she was panting and sweaty, when her pussy was dripping and her skin was smeared with blood.

This night just got a lot more interesting.

"Be ready in twenty minutes," I said and walked out.

There were preparations that needed to be made.

Mina sat fidgeting beside me. Her fingers were twined around the drawstrings of that small bag stuffed with jewelry that sat on her lap, and she kept crossing and uncrossing her legs, which was impossible to ignore.

"Nervous?"

Her gaze shot to me. "No," she lied. "I'm with my bonded. What do I have to be nervous about?"

She watched me with wide lavender eyes, daring me to contradict her. I couldn't. She was right. I would protect her—every instinct in me roared to do just that—and hearing her say it, despite her plan to run. For some reason, my chest felt warm and strange. Even if she was lying, even if her words were more a dare than anything else, hearing her say it made me feel—well, I wasn't sure I could name it. But it wasn't an unpleasant feeling.

We finally reached our destination. The large parking lot was all but empty at this hour but was always watched closely.

Pretender pulled the car over. "Wait here," I said to Mina and got out.

I strode across the lot toward the main doors and had just pushed it open when I heard Mina running after me.

"Wait for me," she called.

I spun back with a snarl. Pretender was chasing after her, and by the look on his face, afraid for his life. As he should be.

I strode forward and grabbed her arm, my gaze sliding to Pretender. "Go back to the car and keep it running."

He nodded and rushed back, and I pulled Mina into the building with me. I gave her a shake. "I allowed you to disobey me back at the apartment because it amused me to do so. When we are out in the open like this, you do not ever defy me, do you understand?"

She tried to pull away from me, her fear real and not mixed with anything else, not this time. "I'm sorry," she whispered.

"Your sorry is meaningless." I took her chin in my hand and tilted her head back. "I am one of The Five. There are beings, not just fae, who would love to discover I have a weakness. You, Mina, are a liability, and running after me the way you did, out in the open for anyone to see, puts us both at risk."

"The lot was deserted," she said, blinking rapidly.

I could smell her threatening tears. The scent of these ones was bitter, not delicious like the ones she'd shed last night while I played with her. I didn't like the scent at all or that she found the need to shed them. "There are cameras all around us," I said through gritted teeth when the urge to snatch her up and take her out of here grew almost impossible to ignore. But doing that would only make this situation worse. Showing how strong my protective instincts were toward her would only show how weak she made me.

She blinked up at me, confused.

"There are members of our race who would love to control me, Mina, and if they thought they could do that by using you, they won't hesitate."

"Oh," she whispered.

That frightened, befuddled look on her face made me want to suck her lower lip into my mouth, to nip it and lap up her blood, to hold her warm soft body against mine while I filled her and fucked her and—

With a growl, I took her hand and led her across the deserted foyer to the elevators. The doors slid closed behind us. It was hard, but I didn't look down at her. We'd be watched in here as well. "Once these doors open, don't speak unless spoken to, understand?"

I felt her looking at me, but if I looked down at her now, in this place, I would give myself away. I would prove she was the weakness they were looking for.

"Do you understand?" I said again, needing to know she understood.

"Yes."

Her voice sounded small. Mina didn't do that—she didn't make herself small, not in the face of the monster she'd been forced to bond with, not for anyone. I didn't fucking like that either.

The doors slid open and I let ice fill my veins as I took her hand and led her into the elders' domain. The room was large, with five doors leading to each of their offices. Cressida, the prime's secretary, sat at her desk in front of his door and glanced up, a cool smile on her face.

Not good. I hadn't expected this meeting to be with the prime. I never would have let Mina come with me tonight if I'd known. Only I dealt with the prime directly when there were special missions. Most of our orders came from lesser elders or the vampire court.

This had just become far more dangerous. "I'm expected," I

said, my voice frigid. She nodded, hitting a button on her desk to let me into his office. "Mina, stay out here with Cressida."

Cressida's smile brightened, eyeing Mina like the vapid piranha she was. "The prime would like to meet her."

Every muscle in my body tightened, but I carefully maintained my unaffected expression as I strode up to the door. Fuck, he had been watching. She'd been seen.

Mina's fingers tightened around mine, seeking reassurance, something I couldn't give her in this place, not with the sharks circling. She squeezed my hand again, and my abdominals clenched like they had earlier, that warmth in my chest returning even stronger than before. I couldn't be warm, not here.

Opening the door, I led Mina in. It was dimly lit like it always was. The ever-present musty, cloying smell filled the room. I didn't need to breathe, and when I was here, chose not to. Mina made a low choking sound at my side, and I squeezed her hand, telling her without words to hold it down.

"Nero," a gravelly voice said.

Mina's gasp was low, but I heard it, which meant the prime had as well. His milky gaze slid to her.

The ancient vampire smiled, flashing yellowed fangs. "What do we have here?"

"Prime," I said, inclining my head. "May I introduce you to my bonded, Mina Kossek," I said, giving her my name to make sure he understood that she was my property and not something he could have or add to his collections.

"*Mina*," he said drawing out her name, then licking his lips. "Come here, female."

Fuck.

She looked up at me, terror in her eyes, and I nodded. I wanted to fucking snarl, to yank her behind me, but showing this male any sign of the possessiveness I felt for her, and how weak she made me, would mean I became this fucker's puppet.

"Nero?" she whispered.

"Go," I said coolly and released her hand, yet I felt anything but cool. I was fucking burning up.

Mina walked to him, trembling. My fangs tingled, and it was only age and control that kept them from sliding down.

The prime grabbed her hips when she reached him, squeezing her flesh, then leaned in and scented her. "You haven't fucked her yet, Nero?"

"Not yet, no." *Fuck*. He could smell the truth on her. I couldn't lie.

"Why?" he asked, his milky gaze sliding back to me.

Any answer I gave would prove she had quickly taken ownership of my fucking spine. "I'm in no hurry," I said.

He released Mina's hips and sat back, his gaze sliding down her bare legs.

"Come here, Mina," I said, and she rushed to my side.

The prime's gaze sliced to me, narrowing. I should have said nothing, but I couldn't fucking stop myself. The only reason he didn't call me on it now was because he wanted me to do something for him. An urgent assignment.

"Go and wait for me in the main office," I said. I needed her out of this room. What had I been thinking? I should have never let her leave my apartment. I should have made Pretender lock the doors when I got out of the car. As soon as she stepped into that parking lot, the prime had seen her. I'd fucked up in a way I couldn't take back. Already the male behind that desk would be plotting.

She rushed out.

The prime watched her go, a calculating look on his face.

Fuck.

Finally, he opened the top drawer of his desk, took out an envelope, and slid it to me. "This needs to be dealt with urgently."

I took it.

He studied me. "Let me know when it's done."

I inclined my head and walked out. Mina rushed to my side as soon as she saw me, and I strode briskly to the elevator.

I kept hold of her hand as we left the building and marched across the lot. Pretender knew better than to get out, and he waited for me to usher Mina into the car. Then he planted his foot, tearing out of the lot.

"What's wrong? What just happened?" Mina asked.

Pretender looked at me in the rearview mirror. "Nero?"

"It was the prime."

"Fuck," my ward muttered.

"He knows what I'm capable of. It's whether he's arrogant enough to test me on it."

The prime wouldn't dare come after Mina, not directly, but he'd be thinking of ways he could use her to get to me, I was positive. Nothing in the past had ever worked. Yet he'd still tried repeatedly.

"Nero, what's going on?"

I snatched her off the seat beside me, pulling her over my lap. Fisting her hair, I tilted her head back and gripped her jaw, my eyes locking on hers. "I made a mistake. I should never have let you come with me. That won't happen again, Mina, do you understand what I'm saying?"

I'd even considered taking her out to dine, away from the apartment, giving her another taste of freedom. Like some smitten, fucking fool trying to impress his female. That wouldn't be happening now.

"You're going to lock me away in that room and never let me out, aren't you?" Her lavender eyes were huge and filled with pain. I *felt* it, fuck, it washed over me. Emotion smashed into me, that anger rushing back that I hadn't felt in so very long. The ice in my veins had melted and now fire seared its way through me instead.

I dragged my nose along her throat, sliding my tongue over the vein fluttering wildly. "You did this to yourself, little doll." Fuck, her scent was making me insane. "Anyone following us?" I asked Pretender.

"No."

If Pretender said we weren't being followed, then we weren't. Besides my brothers, my young ward was the only other being I trusted. His eyes met mine in the mirror, and I nodded.

"You know what happens now, don't you?" I said and scraped my fang along her jaw.

She shivered. "Are you going to punish me?"

"Oh yes. I told you, there'd be a price to pay." The scent of her fear was mixed with desire now, rich and drugging. My little Lalka was just as depraved as me. "I hope you can run in those shoes."

Twelve

MINA

I SHIVERED at the ice in his voice. "Why are you doing this?"

He lifted my purse and hefted its weight. "Disobeying me and putting yourself in danger would be enough to warrant what's about to happen, but attempting to manipulate me so you could try to escape? Well, that can't go unpunished."

Fear and dread coiled with a twisted heat in my lower belly. "I wasn't... I would never—"

"Your attempts to lie to me further only fuel my desire to make you scream, Lalka."

The car pulled over and was immediately engulfed in silence. I couldn't see anything outside. It was too dark.

Nero leaned forward, curling his fingers around my throat. "Do not ever lie to me again, Mina. Not ever."

My mouth was bone dry and my pulse sped so fast, I felt weak-limbed and dizzy, but the cool touch of his skin on mine, his warm breath brushing my lips, had the need between my thighs heightening. What the hell was wrong with me?

He came closer still, so close, his lips brushed mine when he spoke. "You wanted to leave so badly, so now's your chance." He opened the door beside me, pushing it wide.

I shot a look outside. An old building loomed several yards away, and behind it was Oldwood Forest.

"I wouldn't venture into the forest, if I were you. The demons in there won't be as patient with you as I've been."

"You want me to...to run away?" I said as my fear and anticipation grew.

His gaze slid over mine, then dipped to my mouth, my throat, then back up. "That's what you want, isn't it, Mina?"

It had been, after what happened in the club, after making me feel so much only to lock me away again, like I was nothing. Yes, I'd decided to follow Lucinda's lead and try, but I'd needed him, his reassurance, and he'd walked away like I was nothing. I'd doubted that I'd ever break through and reach him, so yes, I'd contemplated leaving, running.

But now? After what happened back in that office, the way Nero had reacted? He hadn't been cold; he'd been furious. I had to hope that meant his emotions were beginning to unravel.

I stared back, locked in place by that ice-cold stare, struggling to form a reply. I couldn't let him win. I wouldn't be some meek, unwanted prisoner who eventually Nero grew bored of and forgot about. My resolve was restored. I wanted a mate. I wanted what my parents have. Maybe Nero was already too far gone, maybe anger was all I'd ever get from him, and he'd never fully regain his ability to feel or to love, but I had to try to coax it from him. I couldn't just give up. I had to at least try.

"Yes," I rasped, telling him the truth. "That's what I wanted. You hurt me, and yes, that made me want to leave you, to never see you again." He wanted honesty, then I'd give it to him. I'd wanted to hurt him or at least affect him the only way I knew how, to make him feel as unwanted as he'd made me feel after he'd touched me, after he'd made me feel more alive than I ever had in my entire life, after giving me hope before ripping it from me and shutting me away like I didn't exist.

His jaw clenched and the muscle there pulsed several times, the ice in his stare melting away like a fire had just been lit inside him and now burned behind his eyes.

I tried to regulate my breathing, but it was impossible as I stared up into the growing inferno blazing down at me. He released me suddenly, and my blood drained from my body, turning me cold.

He sat back in his seat, not looking at me, looking out the window beside him. His chest rose sharply and released on a low growl.

I didn't know what was happening, what I should do—

He turned to me again, and his molten stare scorched across my skin. My blood shot back up from my feet in a hot rush.

"All right, then, now's your chance. Go. Run, little doll," he quietly ordered.

My limbs were trembling and frozen, but I forced them to move, scrambling, stumbling from the back of the car. His dark, humorless laugh echoed from inside as I kicked off my shoes and did as he said—I ran.

Sprinting across the lot, across pitted and broken asphalt that dug into my bare feet, I frantically searched for a place to hide. The forest loomed up ahead, but Nero was right, I'd be a fool to go beyond the tree line. The demons in Oldwood were always on the lookout for breeders, and I wasn't stupid enough to put myself in that position.

The only other option was the huge, dark building looming in front of me. It smelled like wet concrete, iron, and oil. Large sections of the walls were missing, and I bit back a cry as my bare feet came down on something sharp, rocks or glass, as I burst through the nearest opening.

He'd never let me get away, and I realized I didn't want to leave him, not now anyway, but I would keep running because something happened when we played his game. It was twisted and wrong, but somehow it brought us closer together.

I didn't slow when something else cut my foot—my pounding

heart, the adrenaline throbbing through me, wouldn't allow it. I ran past broken and stripped-down pieces of machinery, slipping on the damp oily ground more than once and barely keeping my feet. I sprinted for an open doorway up ahead but slipped on the oily floor again, and this time I went down hard.

Rough concrete scraped my ankle and thigh, snagging and tearing my dress. I barely felt it as I scrambled back to my feet and took off again. He was coming. He was coming for me.

Pinpricks of electricity danced across my skin. The thrill mixed with fear made my scalp tingle and my limbs weak. I gasped for air as my heart pounded out of my chest, and my adrenaline spiked higher and higher without reprieve.

A scraping sound came from somewhere behind me. I pumped my arms harder, faster, while trying to stay quiet, to control my panted breaths. There was another door ahead of me, the moon shining from beyond it. I ran through, then immediately pressed my back against the wall while I tried to control my desperate breaths.

Silence filled the space. There was a hole in the wall across from me, and part of the roof was gone as well, casting everything in a blue glow. Was he out there? Had he walked around the outside of the building instead?

Maybe I should go back the way I came, where it was darker. I was a sitting duck here—

A hand snapped around my throat from behind. I screamed and struggled against Nero's hold. His arm had come around the doorframe; he'd been right behind me. Right there. I'd never lost him, not once.

He was in shadow as he rounded the doorway, and I squirmed and struggled against his hold, clawing at his wrist while he held me against the rough concrete wall.

And gods, the more I struggled, the damper my panties got. He looked down at me and his nostrils flared, scenting me. My face heated because I knew he could smell me. He could smell exactly how this game of cat and mouse we were playing affected me.

Grabbing my wrists, he shoved them over my head. "Got you."

"Did you even give me a head start?" I gasped.

"Oh yes." He leaned in and dragged his nose along my jaw. "Watching you run, your fear so vibrant and wild pouring off you, it does something to me, little doll." He nipped my ear, making me whimper, then lifted his head. "But catching you, the way that makes you so hot and slick, the way you squirm to escape while silently asking me to make you scream my name has frayed the edges of my control to a point I'm not sure I can stop it from breaking."

My panted breaths had turned to gasping sobs of need. What he did to me, what he made me want, *need*, had to be wrong, twisted, but when he held me captive like this, taking from me whatever he wanted, I didn't care. I snapped my fangs at him, egging him on like the wild creature he made me.

I wanted him to break for me, so badly. I wanted him to lose control.

He gathered up my dress, his violet eyes glowing in the moonlight. "Tell me to stop, Mina."

I licked my lips, trembling hard. "Stop," I said, trying to twist from his hold, but there was no escape. I didn't want to escape. "Stop," I said again more forcefully as I held his gaze, silently asking him to take whatever it was he wanted, pleading with him to make me feel as good as he had the last time he'd held me down and touched me.

"Fight harder," he said huskily. "Fight me."

I slammed my legs together and struggled as if my life depended on it, not holding back, crying and pleading, and, oh gods, what was wrong with me that the harder I fought and the tighter he held me, the hungrier I got for his touch, his blood.

I ached so bad, even more than I had all those times he came to my room on my birthdays. He made me feel this way. He'd turned me into this wanton creature who craved fear and pain.

"Give me a word."

"What? What word?"

"I know what you need, but if it gets too much, saying your word will make me stop, will let me know you truly want to."

He could see into the depraved heart of me, and he was going to feed it with his own, but he was giving me a safety net, because Nero would take and take until there was nothing left of me. I could see it in his eyes.

That thought should scare me—instead it made my inner muscles clench. "Pink." It seemed fitting somehow.

The sound of tearing fabric came as soon as the word left my lips. Cool night air hit the damp and swollen flesh between my thighs. Nero forced my legs wide with his body as he covered me there with his hand.

"Scream, little doll," he said, then shoved two long, thick fingers inside me.

I did, I screamed, crying and fighting as he thrust them deep inside me. "Oh gods." I moaned, even as I struggled harder, and the more I struggled, the tighter the tension coiled inside, the deeper and wilder the pleasure rushing up on me grew, and the harder I shook.

"You want to be stuffed full of my cock, don't you, Mina?" he muttered, thrusting faster. The wet sounds coming from between my thighs were lewd, and my begging for him to stop sounded more like what they truly were—pleas for more, like the dirty, brazen creature he made me. "Like you saw in the club. But you want me to hold you down, to force your thighs apart and fuck you into the floor, don't you, Mina?"

I sobbed, shaking harder. "Y-yes." I wanted that so badly. I wanted him to take me, to take it from me.

Nero snarled, then sunk his fangs into my throat. I screamed again, coming around his thrusting fingers as a gush of liquid slid down my thighs. He swiped his tongue over his bite and dropped to his knees in front of me, shoving my dress up to my waist, then buried his face against my swollen flesh, licking and sucking. My knees gave out, but he held me up while he feasted on me in a different way.

I couldn't explain what it was that he did to me, but this was what I wanted, this was what I needed. I didn't want to be someone's princess. I wanted to be held down and used by Nero, by my mate. I wanted him to take pleasure from me, crave me, want only me.

"Please," I begged, wanting all the things he'd said.

His fingers dug deeper into my hips, and he lapped at me in a way that had me fisting his hair and grinding against him. I screamed a second time, holding him to me while he drew out my pleasure, until the deep pulsing convulsions inside me finally stopped and I collapsed.

He scooped me up before I could hit the floor, holding me to his chest. His grip wasn't forceful anymore, it was gentle, almost tender as he carried me through the opening in the wall across from us and around to the lot and his waiting car.

He pressed his mouth against the top of my head. "You did so well, Lalka."

My heart rushed at his words, pleasure of a different kind filling me.

"You pleased me."

I looked up at the chiseled silhouette of his handsome face. "I —I want to please you."

His violet eyes locked on mine. "When I touch you, you like to feel helpless, don't you?" he asked roughly, not a trace of ice in his voice, not anymore.

I nodded, giving him the truth.

His gaze dipped to my lips, then returned to my eyes. "You want your male to use you, to hold you down and take what he wants, don't you, Mina?"

My lips quivered and my eyes stung when I nodded a second time. "There's something wrong with me, isn't there?" I whispered.

He leaned in and pressed his lips to my forehead in a sweet kiss, then looked down at me again and shook his head. "No, my little doll, there is nothing wrong with you. Those desires are what they should be, the antithesis of mine. You run, I chase. You are this way because of me, because you were unlucky enough to be fated to a monster."

Thirteen

NERO

"Don't let her out," I said to Pretender. "No matter how much she complains, not even if she goes on another hunger strike, understand?"

I was leaving in the morning. I'd be gone no more than a week, and if she escaped while I was gone, the chances of me getting to her before someone else did were slim. Someone was always watching and waiting. I was a member of The Five, my identity had been secret until recently, and I'd collected many enemies over the years.

Pretender nodded. "I'll make sure she doesn't leave."

She still had the key she'd stolen and hidden somewhere in her room, so I'd installed a padlock on the outside. She could hate me for it all she wanted, but her safety was more important than anything else. I'd make it up to her somehow when I returned.

"Are you going to tell her you're leaving?" Pretender asked, keeping his gaze averted.

My ward knew I didn't like to be questioned, but he obviously felt strongly enough about it that he'd risked asking. "I assume, you think I should?"

He licked his lips, his gaze darting to me and back down. "I think she'll be calmer knowing you haven't abandoned her, that you're coming back."

"You think my absence would distress her?"

"I do," he said. "I think she might believe you've lost interest in her if you don't tell her why you're leaving."

I slid my hands in my pockets and studied his unnaturally perfect face. "You think you know my bonded better than me?"

His gaze shot to mine. "No, I would never assume to know Mina more than you, sir."

"Then what brings you to this conclusion?" I liked the idea of my little Lalka missing me, craving me, but I doubted she felt strongly enough for me to feel distress at my absence.

His gaze came to me again. "My own feelings. When I was young and new to your home and your employ, you would leave and I'd never know until I sought you out that you were gone. I thought...more than once...that you'd abandoned me the same way my family had."

I stared at him, taken off guard by his confession, and by the mention of his family. He never spoke about them.

"I didn't mean to overstep or imply I knew your female more than you, I assure you I would never—"

"Be at ease, Pretender," I said, the urge to alleviate his disquiet also took me off guard. "I appreciate your candor."

He nodded jerkily.

"I'll go to her now. After you've checked my weapons, you can finish for the evening."

"Thank you," he said and continued to sharpen my favorite blade.

I stopped at the door before I walked out. "I'll see you in a week's time."

His throat worked. "Be safe."

I strode out, a strange feeling in my gut. Pretender had been with me since he was a child, gifted to me by his parents when they were unable to pay their debts and they'd never looked back. He'd been malnourished, terrified, and he'd barely spoken a word when they dumped him at my door. I'd protected and trained him, provided him with an income, a home.

He was the only other being I trusted besides my brothers and, I guessed, the closest thing I'd had to a child of my own. I realized now, for the first time, he probably saw me as a parental figure. I wasn't sure how to process this realization or the accompanying feelings that filled me—feelings that were volatile and unwanted.

But it was too late to stop them now, wasn't it? My little doll had been slowly yet surely melting the ice that had numbed me for so very long.

The fates had decided it was time for the centuries of emotional paralysis to be over. They had something else in store for me now, and even though I'd fought it, I knew from experience that fighting fate was a losing battle.

I stopped outside Mina's door. It was late and she'd be asleep. The agony of resisting her was constant now. I burned for her every hour of the day and night. I was able to withstand the kind of pain lesser males would have gone mad from. The kind of torment that would have driven them to snap and do her damage that could never be repaired or forgiven.

I'd come close to losing that control, more times than should be possible. Only Mina could do that, push me to the edge, and only she had the power to stop me. I realized now, the primal instinct to mate was just as powerful as the need to protect her, even from myself.

Nothing could make me hurt my little doll. I knew that now.

Sliding the key from my pocket, I undid the padlock soundlessly and opened the door.

I'd suffered the kind of torture that shattered the most powerful of men. I never believed anything could break me after surviving that—I'd been wrong.

Mina could break me, into a million pieces, and she didn't even know it.

Gods, I craved her love like a starved beast, even if I didn't know how the emotion felt any longer, even though I didn't know if I was even capable of ever returning it. All I knew was I wanted it, because I needed her to want only me. Only then could I be sure I'd never lose her, that she would never leave me.

You will never know what it feels like to be loved by me, because I could never love a monster like you.

The words she'd said that first night in the garden echoed through my mind. Did she still feel that way? Was I still that same monster in her eyes?

I closed the door behind me and approached my sleeping bride. She was covered in a mountain of blankets, her breathing slow and even, but it quickened when I got closer to her. Even in sleep she sensed me, wanted me.

Would my leaving truly distress her?

Watching the rapid rise and fall of her chest under the covers, I slid my hand down the front of my shirt, undoing the buttons as I went.

She groaned in her sleep, shoving back the covers, and her scent washed over me. She was rubbing her thighs together while she muttered and moaned in her sleep, telling me how much she needed me.

I needed her as well. I just wanted another taste of her before I left. A week without her felt like an eternity, and the mere thought stunned me. I shrugged off my shirt and stripped off the rest of my clothes.

I breathed her scent deep into my lungs as I lifted the covers, then eased onto the mattress beside her. Anticipation was coursing through me. Something else I hadn't felt in too long to remember.

I wanted to fuck her, badly, but I wouldn't, not tonight, not right before I left—not when I didn't have days to glut on her like the starved monster she made me.

This would have to do until I returned.

~

Mina

A strong arm banded around me, while a hand clamped over my mouth.

I tried to scream behind cold fingers, to get free, but I was held too tight.

"Fight all you want, Lalka, you will never escape me," Nero growled against my ear.

As soon as I heard his voice, a wave of desire washed over me, but I was already hot and needy, wasn't I? I'd been dreaming of him. Of Nero here with me, of him catching me, touching me. That's when I became aware of his bare skin against my back. My nightgown had lifted while I slept, and I could feel every hard, cool inch of him pressed against my body.

Something hard prodded my bottom. His cock. "Your word, Mina?"

My breath shook from me. We were going to play our game.

"Say it so I know you remember it."

"Pink."

"And if you're unable to speak, hit me three times in quick succession and I'll stop."

"Why wouldn't I be able to speak?"

"Tell me you understand?"

I shivered, feeling unsure, but also full of anticipation. "I understand."

He released me suddenly, and excitement rushed through my body as I immediately dove for the edge of the bed. Nero grabbed me by the ankle and dragged me back, while I kicked and fought. He shoved my legs wide, and came down on top of me, grinding against me.

My underwear was the only barrier between us and I gasped. "No," I cried. "Stop."

He chuckled. "How loud will you scream, do you think, when I fuck you for the first time? Will you cry and writhe and beg for more when I finally fill that tight little pussy and claim what's mine?"

I whimpered, his dirty words, and his big body covering me, grinding on me, made it hard to think, let alone breathe. I tried to lift my hips to chase the feeling quickly building inside me.

"My shameless little doll," he said, pinning my hands over my head.

His eys held mine as he started moving his hips in a way that had my eyes rolling back in my head.

It didn't take long before he had me crying out, shaking and groaning for him as he pushed me over the edge, and before I could catch my breath, Nero lifted me off the mattress and shoved me against the pink velvet headboard. My back was to the fabric, my legs out in front of me. He climbed to his knees, one on either side of my thighs, and I shoved at him, still playing our game, as his cock jutted from him right in front of my face.

I'd never seen it up close before, and I wanted to touch it, badly.

He fisted my hair and jerked my head back, making me watch as he bit down on his palm, then slid his bloody hand along his hard length, coating himself in blood.

My mouth watered and a needy whimper slipped free. He was going to make me do what I saw others doing in his club.

"Open your mouth," he demanded.

He was going to use my mouth for his pleasure. I shook my head, slamming my lips together, while my fear of what was about to happen mixed with the thrill of it all and my longing for the taste of his blood. He jammed his thumb in the side of my mouth, forcing it open and, ignoring my punching and scratching, gripped his hard length and pushed it into my open mouth.

Saltiness mixed with the decadent flavor of his blood hit my tongue, and his scent was deeper, muskier now.

"Wrap your lips around me, little doll, while your bonded fucks your pretty mouth."

I stopped hitting and dug my fingers into his hard thighs when he pushed deep, hitting the back of my throat. I gagged. "Relax your throat, Mina," he said huskily. "Let me in."

I swallowed convulsively, and he groaned and started thrusting. He was thick, and my mouth was stretched impossibly wide, so wide my jaw already ached. He was too long to fit all of him in, but I wanted to please him. I wanted to make him feel good, like he had done for me.

"Eyes on me," he said, tugging on my hair.

I did as he said, my eyes locking on his, and just the sight of his violet eyes, hot and hungry, had me moaning and squeezing my thighs tightly together.

"That's it, Lalka. Suck off every drop of my blood." He cupped my face with his other hand and ran his thumb along my jaw while he thrust into my mouth over and over. "You're doing so good."

His touch was gentle, tender, a complete contrast to the way he filled my mouth. How could I love this? How could I want it? But I did. I'd never felt so wanted in my life.

"I'm going to come down your throat, and you're going to swallow every drop, understand?" he said huskily.

I didn't know what that meant, but I would do it, whatever it was. I wanted to make him happy. The saltiness intensified, something was leaking from the tip.

"When I say bite, sink those little fangs into my cock, Mina."

Oh gods. I nodded.

Nero gripped my hair even tighter, his cock growing thicker, making me whimper. He pulled out, so only the swollen head was in my mouth. "Bite," he said. I did, biting into the firm flesh. "Now release." I did, and he snarled and thrust deep again into my mouth, flooding it with blood and something else. His come.

"Swallow," he growled.

I gulped, but there was too much, and it slipped from my mouth, sliding down my chin, while he continued to thrust.

Nero finally slowed, and with his eyes still on me, he slid from my mouth. Swiping his thumb over my chin, he collected what I'd spilled and pushed it back past my lips. "All of it. Suck it clean."

I did, eagerly.

"Do you like the way your bonded tastes?" he asked as he watched closely, his nostrils flaring as I lapped up every drop.

"Yes," I whispered, my voice hoarse. "Very much."

His chest expanded on an unneeded breath. "How slick are your thighs?"

I slid them together. "Very." I looked down and gasped. His cock was still hard, thrusting from his hips, large and intimidating.

Hooking me around the waist, he pulled me down the bed and rolled me to my side, so my back was to him, then he covered me, pushing my hips forward so I was half on my stomach. I tried to pull away, but he curled a hand around my throat and gripped my hip with the other.

He yanked my underwear down my legs, tossing them aside, then his cock was prodding me from behind, and he shoved it between my slick thighs. It parted my pussy, rubbing over the place he liked to use his fingers, but not going inside me.

"Squeeze your thighs together, nice and tight," he said roughly against my ear.

I did as he said, moaning as he started to thrust between my clenched thighs. One hand left my hip and covered my mouth. "Bite," he demanded.

I did, sinking a fang into the finger he pushed past my lips. Blood bubbled up and dripped from the tip. Before I could lap it up, he slid his hand under me, cupping me and using his bloody finger to ease the way as he slid it between my folds, making it extra slippery as he rubbed. *Oh gods. So good.* I was already past excited, and when he touched me, I couldn't hold in my plea for more.

"Please, Nero. I need it."

"Who do you belong to, Mina?"

I gasped when he rubbed faster, pushing the swirl of tension building inside me higher. "You. Oh gods, only you make me feel this way."

He slammed against my bottom, thrusting faster, his hard length teasing my sensitive flesh. "That's right. And no one else will ever touch this cunt, little doll, no one else will ever make you scream, and if they do, I will fucking kill them."

He sank his fangs into my throat, and I screamed, coming instantly. He thrust twice more, groaning against my skin, and then he pulsed between my thighs, coating them with his come.

His hand slid from my throat, down to my breast, and he massaged as he sucked gently, while he continued to feed from me.

I loved it, all of it.

Finally, he lapped at my skin, sealing his bite. His weight vanished, then I was rolled again and pulled up against him. His arms were still a little stiff when they came around me, when he held me like last time, but my heart filled, because he was trying.

"I have to leave for a while," he said into the darkness.

I froze, trying to pull away. "You're leaving me?" I hated how pathetic I sounded, but there was no holding in the way I felt.

He didn't let me go. "I won't be gone long. A week at most."

"Then take me with you."

"I can't do that. It'll be too dangerous."

"Does this have to do with your meeting with the prime?"

"Yes."

I remembered the last time he'd visited me at my parents' house, late at night, and two days late. He'd smelled of blood, his and someone else's. "Are you going to kill someone?"

"Yes," he said without hesitation. "There is a risk to us, not just to our people, but to you, because you belong to me." He tilted my head back, his touch more gentle than it had ever been. "I have enemies, Mina, because of who I am and what I've done. Enemies who would love to hurt me."

"How can they hurt you? Nothing hurts you," I said, because it was the truth. My fated mate wasn't capable of feeling for me the way I realized I was starting to feel for him.

"Word will have gotten out about the blood moon ceremony. About the little female who I keep locked away, protecting her from anyone who would harm her." He shook his head, and a look passed over his face, one of surprise. "I should never have claimed you. I should have walked away the day I found you."

Dread filled me. Was he going to send me away. "You don't want me anymore, do you?"

"I want you more than ever, Lalka. I should never have claimed you because I'm not fooling anyone, not even myself, not anymore." He searched my face. "You are melting my heart, little doll. I don't know what I feel for you, but I feel something, for the first time in centuries...I feel *something*, and that makes you incredibly dangerous."

He cared about me. "Just...please, don't send me away," I rushed out.

"I couldn't even if I wanted to. Even knowing it would be the safest thing for both of us. But I can't do it."

His tone, his expression was stoic, even cold as usual, but the words were anything but. His heart may be melting, but he'd been emotionless for so long, the warmth hadn't yet touched the surface. "What do you need me to do?"

"I need you to stay in this room while I'm gone. I need to know you are here and safe." He ran the backs of his fingers down the side of my face. "I've killed more beings than I can count. My enemies are vast, and some of them are closer than I would like. I'm a valuable asset because I've eliminated every target I've been given. I've withstood months or brutality and torture. I'm the weapon our elders wield when one is needed."

"You were tortured?"

Another brush of his cool fingers down the side of my face. "Yes."

"Is that how your heart stopped?"

He gently slid his thumb over my lower lip. "Yes."

I couldn't bear the thought of it. Who was he before all the death and pain? Nero had buried that part of himself deep under layers of ice. It would take a long time to uncover that male again —if it were even possible.

"The previous fae monarch still has supporters, members of his royal house who fled when the new king was crowned, and they're looking for revenge."

"You killed the old king, didn't you?"

"Yes," he said, watching his own hand as it slid over my shoulder. "I killed him." His gaze lifted to mine. "No one deserved death as much as him. Vampire and fae have been enemies so long, I think most don't even remember why."

"I read in one of the history books in my parents' library that the king abducted a vampire," I said. "Is that true?"

His throat worked. "Yes, he did. He took Dorotha."

"Your sister?"

"She'd been young and innocent, breakable...a lot like you, my little Lalka. Back then, our people and theirs had coexisted, somewhat peacefully. Until the king snatched her and made her his breeder."

"What?" I whispered in horror.

"Back then, before advancements had been made in that area, childbirth was extremely dangerous for the fae—they often lost their children and their females. Vampires didn't have the same problems, our numbers were growing, our females strong. So in an attempt to strengthen their bloodline, the king ordered the males in the royal house to take a vampire breeder to bear their young. Vampire and fae are both blood drinkers, both strong, immortal, so they used us, they used our females...they held them captive and forced them to bear their young."

That part had been missing from my schoolbooks, of course. I couldn't imagine how terrified those females must have been. "I had no idea."

"War broke out between our people as a result, lasting many lifetimes. That whole time, my sister had been hidden away, and I'd never been able to find her. Eventually, the king killed her to punish me for the part I'd played in the war, for all the fae I killed in her name. Then he left her body for me to find."

"That's...so awful, Nero. It's sick and twisted and evil. I'm so sorry."

He searched my eyes, then dipped his chin. "Yes, it is all of those things. The war may have ended after I killed the king and the treaty was signed, but the danger is still there, it's just different. The Five leaving the fae border and stepping away from that life has the elders nervous. We're powerful, and they want to regain control over us, but especially over me."

I frowned. "You're still helping them, though. You're going away now because of the prime's order. You're already doing as they ask."

He nodded. "Refusing the prime is not done, Mina, not by anyone, but I could. I could refuse, I could challenge him, I could walk away, and that's what he's most afraid of. He wanted me to stay in the shadows. He wants to put me back there more than anything. If he'd known about you earlier, and my intention to claim you, he would have used you to get his way."

"And you think he'd use me now?"

"If given the chance. Bonding with a female, mating, those things change a male, especially one like me. It could make me... unpredictable, even more dangerous. But coming for you now would be signing his own death warrant. The prime is arrogant, and I don't trust him, but coming for you would be going directly against our sacred laws. Even he isn't above them." His violet eyes darkened. "Still, I want you to promise me, while I'm gone, that you will stay in here. Pretender will spread the word that I've sent you away. Better for everyone to believe you're not here at all than risk your safety."

"I promise I'll stay in this room."

He pulled me up his body, so I was curled on his lap. "Thank you," he said. "Now, you need to feed, Lalka. I've left blood for you, but I need you to drink your fill before I leave."

"Okay." I snuggled in closer and nuzzled his throat, finding the thick pulsing vein there, while he rubbed my back—then I bit him.

And I fed from my male.

Fourteen

NERO

The camp was up ahead.

Light from the fire flickered over the faces of the fae warriors as they stared into the flames, blood still smeared on their chins and hands from their last meal. Animal carcasses and a few other creatures that lived in this forest lay rotting around their camp, along with piles of ash from the demons who'd gotten too close and paid with their heads.

It had taken me four days to track them here. They'd covered their movements well as they'd moved along the border. I'd had to go slow, and I'd taken more than one unnecessary detour.

I studied the fae soldiers sitting around the fire. I knew them all. I'd been tortured by most of them at the command of the old king. When I'd finally escaped, there'd been nothing left of my humanity. I'd been numb, broken in so many ways that my heart had stopped beating.

Even then, even as cold as I'd been after what had happened to me, I'd never lost my thirst for revenge. Killing the old king for what he'd done to my sister had taken centuries, but I'd done it.

I'd avenged Dorotha.

My chest ached at the thought of her, and I tried to rub away the new sensation.

I hadn't had the strength to kill them then after my escape.

I did now.

What was left of the old king's fae guard were holed up deep in the forest, still close to the border between our territory and theirs. They'd fled, but they'd stayed close, not straying far from home. The prime said they'd been spotted in the city, which was why I'd been sent to track and kill them, but finding them all the way out here, I wasn't sure I believed they'd ever left this place.

Yes, I was going to execute them. I'd dreamed of murdering them since the day I escaped, since I found my sister's beaten and bloody body. Killing these males was the only way to ensure peace remained between our people and the new fae royal house, but the prime inferring that they were an imminent threat to us, to the elders themselves, seemed unlikely since they obviously hadn't traveled far from the border at all.

The prime was playing fucking war games and had held back important information. What was his endgame?

Drawing two of my knives from their sheaths, I let them fly, taking out two guards I didn't recognize. Their bodies thumped to the ground, and the others exploded to their feet. Sliding my favorite blade free, I stepped from the trees. "Gentlemen, it's been a while," I said and flashed my fangs.

The fae drew their swords, but they couldn't win, not when they were malnourished from drinking animal blood, and not at full strength. I ran at them, a blur of speed, slicing their throats, and removing their heads one at a time, their bodies falling limp to the ground like dominos.

Their deaths were too fast, too easy, after what they'd done to Dorotha at the king's orders, but for once, death and vengeance wasn't the most important thing to me—getting back to Mina outweighed what had driven me for longer than I could remember.

My feelings for my bonded may be a weakness and extremely

dangerous, but there was no stopping it—and the days apart from her had made it clear that my bride had invaded every part of me, that she'd all but conquered me completely.

I needed to make sure there were no others along the border before I returned to her, because now that I'd spilled fae blood, those close by would know and they'd be coming. I couldn't risk any of them following me home to her.

Another day at most to take care of any others, then I would return to my Lalka.

~

Mina

I stared up at the ceiling, unable to sleep.

Nero had been gone four long nights. I missed him. There was no point trying to deny it or pretend otherwise. I missed my bonded male, I missed my mate. No, he hadn't made me his in truth yet, but that didn't matter. My heart didn't care about that. He was mine.

I rolled to my side, curling around the pillow he'd used, breathing in his scent, and closed my eyes, to try and sleep—

There was a crash against my door. I shot up in bed as a feral growl came from beyond it, along with more thumps and crashes.

The sound of the lock turning came next. I jumped off the bed, scrambling back as the door was shoved open.

Two large vampires walked in. One of them dragging Pretender in behind him, bloody and beaten. Gods, his face was almost unrecognizable, his body misshapen from dislocated limbs and broken bones. Whoever these males were, they meant to do me harm and Pretender fought hard to protect me.

They were Nero's enemies, the ones he'd told me about.

The male holding Pretender dumped him on the ground.

Pretender reached a hand toward me, choking on his own blood—still trying to protect me even now.

Another vampire walked in.

I gasped and scrambled back until I hit the wall.

The prime.

The ancient male's rheumy gaze slid over me, and he smiled. "Ah, there you are, Mina. Your friend here wouldn't share your whereabouts. We had to search every nook and cranny in this place to find you." He held out his hand. "Come here, child."

I shook my head. "I'm not going anywhere with you."

"Nero told me to come and get you. He won't be back for some time. You need protection."

Pretender made a gurgling sound, struggling to get to his hands and knees. One of the prime's guards slammed a booted foot down on his back, pinning him to the ground.

A cry burst from me. "Please...stop. Don't hurt him anymore."

"Then come here," the prime said.

"Nero... H-he told me to stay here," I said, my voice shaking as hard as my limbs. "That I wasn't to leave."

"Nero didn't realize the scope of the assignment I sent him on. Now he does, and I am to provide you with safe accommodation until his return."

Pretender hissed, sounding wild.

"I don't believe you," I rasped.

"You dare defy your prime?" one of the guards barked at me. "Nero is beholden to our prime, as are you." He slid a wicked-looking knife from its sheath and dropped to his knees. Fisting Pretender's hair, he wrenched his head back, knife to his throat. "Come easy or Nero's ward dies."

"Don't hurt him!" What choice did I have? But I wasn't stupid. They were trying to make me believe Nero wanted this, but I knew they were lying.

"I'll come, just please, don't hurt him anymore." Pretender was the first friend I'd had in so long, and he was important to Nero. I'd never let anyone hurt him.

"Wise choice," the prime said, and again held out his hand.

I took it, a shudder moving though me when his cold, clammy skin touched mine. The ancient male stopped beside Pretender and nudged him with his boot. "Your attempts to protect her were valiant, if misplaced." He smiled wide, flashing his yellowing fangs. "I am prime, and I take what I want. Nero won't mind if I use her first." He gave my hand a brutal squeeze, making me wince. "If he does, well, he'll just have to get over it."

That's when what he'd just said registered. *Use me?*

I tried to pull from his hold again. I'd rather die than let this monster use me in any way. He squeezed my hand tighter, so tightly I cried out in pain and my legs almost buckled beneath me.

"Fighting will only make it worse for you," he said, then towed me from the room, while Pretender dragged his broken and bloody body toward the door, hissing and growling and trying to follow.

NERO

I'D BEEN RIGHT. There were camps all along the border. I was beginning to believe the prime knew exactly what he was doing when he sent me on this mission.

I'd been fighting all day. As I thought, there were others camping close by, and they'd come for me.

Now I was covered in my enemy's blood and surrounded by bodies. The old royal house needed to be cleared out to ensure peace prevailed, but the new king could have sent his own warriors to do this.

Something wasn't right. This wasn't my fight. I shouldn't even be here. Was the prime trying to reignite a war? Or had he used this mission as a distraction to keep me occupied? To get me out of the way?

Surely he wouldn't go after Mina. Surely he wasn't so arrogant and stupid that he believed he was above our laws, that I'd let him get away with harming her in any way.

"Fuck."

I'd underestimated him.

That's exactly what he was planning.

He'd decided to go after Mina. He'd known about her before

we'd even walked into his office. This had always been the plan. Of course, it had. I spun and ran at top speed through the forest toward the city. How could I have been so blind?

My phone vibrated in my pocket, and I quickly pulled it out.

Wet coughing echoed down the line before I could say anything.

I slowed. "Pretender?"

"M-Mina."

"Where is she?" I already knew, though, didn't I?

"P-Prime... He came for her."

With a snarl, I shoved my phone back in my pocket, ducked my head, and exploded through the trees. The prime had made his move in an attempt to control me. He'd taken my female.

He truly thought his position as prime would protect him. That he could commit the most heinous crime one vampire could commit against another, and that our ancient laws wouldn't apply to him. He was so very fucking wrong.

His position would not protect him, not now. Not from me. He would die for this, they all would.

How quickly that death was depended on the condition my Lalka was in when I finally got to her.

Mina

"You're still a virgin," the prime said and licked his thin lips. "I can't wait to taste you."

I stood in a grand room, a formal living room, full of priceless antiques, art, and furniture that looked pretty but no doubt felt like a bed of nails to sit on, and stared at the terrifying male, swallowing down the acid curdling in my stomach. How could he know that?

"I can smell it, Mina," he said as if he'd read my mind. "A

female's scent is different once she's been claimed by her mate. His scent blends with hers. Once he's been inside her, he seeps from her pores." He licked his lips again. "Nothing tastes quite as good as virgin blood."

A shudder went through me, and I curled my fingers into tight fists, my nails digging into flesh. "What are you going to do?"

"Oh, that will be a surprise, lovely Mina. Now you'll go with Gretchen here, and she will prepare you for this evening's festivities." His red, glistening tongue slid along one pointed fang. "It will be a night none of us will ever forget."

I turned to the female, Gretchen, when she lightly took my elbow. She looked pale, her gaze downcast. She couldn't even look me in the eyes. She was just as terrified of the prime as I was.

As soon as she led me from the room, I grabbed her arm. "Please, you have to help me."

Her eyes shot up to me, and she shook her head, tilting her head toward the room we'd just walked out of. The prime was old and incredibly strong, and going by the fear in Gretchen's eyes, might still be able to hear us.

I shut my mouth and let her direct me down a wide hall, around a corner, then turning into another.

"Will you help me, please?" I said when I thought we were far enough away.

Her eyes met mine again, and they were filled with regret, and fear. "I'm sorry. He'll kill me if I even try."

Whatever this was, letting me go would put her in serious danger, would mean punishment or worse.

My mouth went dry, fear prickling over my skin like tiny pointed needles. "What is he going to do to me?"

She stopped by a door and quickly let us in. It was a large bedroom, as opulent as the rest of the house. I hated it. Gretchen started toward the open door on the other side of the room, and I grabbed her arm, stopping her again.

"Please. Tell me?"

Her gaze darted to the closed bedroom door, then back. "Tonight, the first night, y-you will be presented to the...the elders."

"What will happen? Why am I being presented to the elders?"

She shook her head. "I'm not permitted to say, Mina. I'm so sorry. You will survive this. I promise. You will get through this."

"They did this...whatever this is, to you, didn't they?"

Her spine stiffened, and she looked away. "Come, we need to prepare you."

"I won't do it. I won't go."

She turned back to me then, and there was pity in her eyes. "They won't give you a choice."

This was the prime, the elders, they were all powerful. No one could help me. No one could stop this, not even Nero. The prime's word was law.

Whatever was about to happen, I had to endure. If I wanted to go home to Nero, I just had to survive this.

I pulled my knees up to my chest, wrapping my arms around them. The raw linen of my smock was rough against my cheek, just as it was against the rest of me. It smelled fresh, as if I could still smell the field the cotton came from. It hadn't been washed or treated with any harsh chemicals. The soap and shampoo Gretchen had told me to use had been the same, no scent.

The only scents on my body were my own.

I curled my toes into the damask fabric under me, pushing deeper into the chair as my stomach clenched hard. Gretchen left me in this room after that, locking me in, and told me someone would come for me when it was time. That was several hours ago.

As much as I wanted to, there was no use lying to myself anymore. I knew what this all meant for me. The prime was going to feed from me.

Most vampires hated unnatural or strong chemical scents. It interfered with their enjoyment of feeding, filling their senses and distorting the flavor of the blood they were drinking. My father used to hate it when my mother wore any kind of perfume or used scented soap.

The prime had said himself he couldn't wait to taste me, and it was happening tonight.

The lecherous, repulsive old creep was going to drink my blood. I bit down on my lip when a moan of horror tried to slip past my trembling lips. My blood wasn't his to drink, it was Nero's. Only Nero's.

You have to do this. There's no getting out of it.

I wanted to run, to escape this place, to find Nero and hide— but there was no escaping the prime.

Besides, this place was swarming with guards and security cameras. I'd seen the cameras in the halls and several guards out the window. I wouldn't get far even if I did somehow manage to get out of this room.

A loud knock had me jolting in the chair. The door opened and a large male walked in. I jumped to my feet and backed up until I hit the wall behind me. The male strode forward with a smirk, then grabbed my arm. "Let's go."

He dragged me from the room, marching me down the halls, turning one corner after another. This place was huge and cold and soulless. For the first time since Nero took me to his home, I longed for my little pink room. I wanted to be there with him more than anything.

I screamed his name in my mind, as if I could somehow reach him that way, as if he might hear me and come for me. But that wasn't how this worked, and even if I could reach him through our bond, I doubted it would even work because we weren't mated yet.

My escort stopped in front of a door, shoved it open, and dragged me into a large, dim, candlelit room. The glow from the candles should have made it feel warm, but it didn't. It was cold and frigid and as devoid of a soul as the rest of this place.

A large, mahogany dining table stood in the center of the room, and my escort dragged me to it. He grabbed me unceremoniously and lifted me off my feet. I shrieked and fought as he laid me on the tabletop. Gretchen appeared at his side and tied my wrist down while he held me immobile. They moved around the table quickly, until my wrists and ankles were pinned down.

Gretchen didn't meet my eyes as she lit several more candles around the room, then quickly left, leaving me alone and utterly helpless, stretched out on the table like a side of roasted beef.

I was breathing hard and fast, my head spinning from the blood pumping forcefully through my veins. My throat was impossibly dry, too dry to scream, and sweat prickled over my skin.

The sound of footsteps came from beyond the door, not just one set, several. A moment later the door opened again and the prime walked in, followed by the other four elders. One by one their cold, hungry eyes sliced to me. My stomach lurched as ice-cold terror slid through me. My blood froze in my veins and my world spun as if my very soul had tried to lurch from my body in a desperate bid to escape this horror. But that wasn't possible. I was stuck here. There was no escape for me.

I tugged at my binds as the elders closed in and positioned themselves around the table, one at each foot, and the other two at my wrists. The prime strode to the head of the table, standing so close to me that his stomach brushed the top of my head.

"It has been a long time, brothers, since we have received such a gift. The position of prime, of esteemed elders, has stood long before our laws were created. These positions of power have existed since our creation, and since that time, virgin blood was offered for our nourishment, as our right as the most exalted members of our race. And as such, we are not beholden or tied by laws. We are above them. And tonight we take the blood of this female as is our due. We thank our loyal servant, Nero, for this offering, for gifting us such a sweet virgin to feast upon this night."

The others made approving sounds, their sharp, hungry eyes moving over me.

Nero didn't gift me to these monsters. These males were so used to getting what they wanted, without repercussions, that they just assumed Nero wouldn't make a fuss, that he might be angry but he'd accept that they'd abducted his bonded and tortured her this way, or at least, that he had no way to stop them, to stop this. They truly believed they could control him.

The prime slid one of his long, sharp fingernails down my throat to the top of my smock, then sliced through the fabric. As soon as he made the first cut in the linen, the other four grabbed at it, shredding it with their nails, tearing it from me and exposing my body, as if they were skinning fresh meat to be devoured.

"Please, no...don't—"

The prime grabbed my jaw. "You do not speak," he hissed, giving my head a rough shake before his gaze lifted. "Brothers, feast."

The ancient males all lurched forward, one by one, latching on to me with their long yellowed fangs, sinking them deep into my flesh. Pain lashed through me instantly, so horrific that no sound left me when I opened my mouth to scream. My body bowed on the table, suspended, locked in agony. The prime jerked my head to the side, and he sunk his fangs into my throat.

A scream burst from me then, forced from deep inside me, raw and guttural, like a tortured animal.

They chose to make me scream in agony rather than pleasure. When a vampire fed, it was their choice, and every male at this table had chosen pain.

But as excruciating as this was, I was glad of it. Being forced to feel pleasure during this would have been far more horrific. I would rather this feeling of being torn apart than the alternative.

My stomach heaved, and I lost control of my body, vomiting on the table as my bladder released, both pooling beneath me.

The five ancient vampires seemed to get even more excited by it, their fangs tearing from my flesh only to sink in again, deep into my thighs, my waist, my breasts.

The warmth seeped from my limbs, and they grew heavy, pins and needles starting at the tips of my fingers and toes. Swirling darkness creeped in from the corners of my eyes as I struggled to keep them open.

Let go. Stop fighting it.

The sooner I let the darkness take me, the sooner this would be over.

Sixteen

NERO

My knees almost fucking buckled under me from a wave of emotion smashing into me. *Mina.* It was coming to me through our blood bond. I'd never felt it like this before. I'd purposely closed myself off to it, but I felt it now like I was being battered by a raging storm.

My female was suffering. She was in unbearable agony.

The monster inside me roared louder, bursting to the surface. I was going to kill them all. I was going to tear them to shreds and watch as they bled out at my feet.

The bond was strengthening with every passing moment. It was as if Mina were tugging on it, as if she were calling out to me.

I'm coming, Lalka. Hang on. Please, hang on a little longer.

I knew where I needed to go before I hit the city. Instead of going to the prime's apartment, I stayed on the outskirts of Roxburgh, heading toward his weekend house. It would take half an hour by car. I could halve that on foot, but I still might not be fast enough to get to her in time.

I focused on the pull and flex of my muscles as I dug deeper, pushing harder, forcing myself to run at speeds I'd never reached in my life, until the huge mansion finally loomed ahead.

I snarled, and the sound, the feeling, was like lightning cracking deep inside me. It exploded from my gut, heat searing through my veins and throbbing in my chest.

I'm almost there, Lalka.

Two of the prime's guards ran at me as I approached. I pulled my knife free, buried it in the chest of the one closest, then slashed the blade down his front, spilling his insides, then spun to the second male and used my fangs to tear out his throat, barely slowing my stride.

No one and nothing would stop me from getting to Mina.

Kicking in the door, I hacked through the two guards standing there and let the connection to my little doll lead me. The prime didn't need a heavy guard, not in the house, because no one challenged the elders and the twisted things they did. The prime was used to doing whatever the fuck he liked and getting away with it.

He did what he wanted. He *took* whatever the fuck he wanted.

Not anymore.

He would pay the price for breaking our laws just like everyone else.

I rounded the corner at the end of a hall, and Gretchen, one of the prime's servants, stood at a door with another guard. The female was silently crying, her shoulders shaking uncontrollably.

The male beside her stepped forward when he saw me, pulling his weapon. I knocked it from his hand and wrenched his head from his body. Gretchen cowered, trembling, but made no sound. She jerked back as I grabbed and lifted her out of the way. "Leave and don't come back," I growled.

She immediately spun and sprinted away.

Gripping the handles, I forced myself to slow down and open the doors as soundlessly as possible.

They swung open, and the sight before me decimated what remained of the ice I'd lived under for so long. It shattered, and the monster inside me, the wild thing, broke free after so many centuries of being buried.

Mina was tied down on a table, her dress torn from her, her naked body deathly pale and covered in bite marks. Her skin was smeared with blood, while the five elders fed from her, unaware of what was going on around them, blood drunk from gorging on my female, from hurting her, draining her.

Mina lay there unmoving, unblinking. No fight left in her. The sound of her heartbeat had slowed dangerously. The elders had lost control completely. They were killing her.

Baring my teeth, I ran to the nearest one, wrenched back his head, and tore it off. I moved with speed to the next and the next, until only the prime was left standing. Like the others, he was too blood drunk, blinded by his hunger, to notice what was going on around him.

"Prime," I roared.

The older male blinked, breaking from his trance, and slid his fangs from Mina's throat.

He lifted his head, finally looking around him. He blinked again several times, as he took in the decapitated remains of the four other elders—then his gaze sliced back to me.

"How dare you," he seethed, Mina's blood spraying from his red lips. "You will be put to death for this. You will—"

"No," I snarled. "You are the one who will die." In the blink of an eye, I closed the distance between us and grabbed the ancient vampire by the throat. He tried to toss me away, and any other day, he would have succeeded. He was older, stronger, but I was fueled by rage, the kind only a male protecting his female possessed. Right then, I matched his strength and then some. I squeezed the prime's throat with everything I had, and he dropped to his knees, gasping.

I wanted to take my time torturing him, peeling the skin from his body, slicing and pulverizing until he begged me for death. I wanted to hear him scream. But my need for revenge came second to the needs of my female, and she needed me. Now.

His mouth opened and closed like a suffocating fish as he

clawed at my wrist. I grinned down at him as I dug my nails into his papery skin—pushing deep until I could grip his spine, then I tore it out through his throat and tossed it aside. His lifeless body fell to the floor, and I kicked him out of the way and rushed to Mina's side.

There was so much fucking blood. I quickly swiped my tongue over the gaping wound in her throat where blood still oozed, then gently, I took her precious face in my hands and turned her toward me. She was cold, her gaze dull, lifeless, staring straight ahead.

"Lalka?" Her pulse was slow, sluggish. She needed to feed.

Quickly I snapped the ropes around her wrists and ankles, then worked my way around her, licking the open bites all over her body, sealing them. She didn't make a sound, didn't move, just continued to stare blindly at nothing.

"It's going to be okay. No one can hurt you now." I swiped my tongue across the side of her waist, sealing the last bite and stopping the bleeding. "I'm going to lift you now, Lalka. I'm sorry if it causes you pain, but I need to feed you."

She said nothing.

I lifted her carefully, still the pain must have been unbearable, but she remained limp, soundless. I carried her over to a chair and sat with her across my lap. "Drink, my love. You need to feed."

Her head lay against my shoulder. She was too weak to fucking lift it. Sliding my arm free, I nicked the vein in my throat, just a small slice because she'd have to start slow and build up her strength. Lifting her higher, I cupped the back of her head and pressed her mouth to the cut.

She made a small whimpering sound, and I felt her tongue press against it with a barely there touch. I wanted her out of this place, I needed to get her out of here, but I was afraid if I waited any longer to feed her, I'd fucking lose her.

I'd just killed the elders, murdered all five of them in the prime's own residence. I didn't regret it. I'd do it again. But I didn't know what that would mean for me, or for Mina. If we had to run, we would. I had more than enough money to protect and care for her anywhere in the world. I could take her wherever she wanted to go.

Which was why I needed to get her out of here. I needed to get her to safety.

Her lips moved, soft like butterfly wings against my skin, then she sucked gently. Relief filled me. I couldn't remember the last time I felt this way. "That's it." I rubbed her slender back, encouraging her to drink more. "Don't stop, Mina."

The seal of her lips grew firmer, and her hand slid up my chest to curl around the side of my throat. More relief rolled through me, so strong, so overwhelming, I shook from the sensation. Her legs curled up, her toes digging into my thigh—then she struck, going deeper.

Her fangs sunk into my vein, her nails into my shoulder, and she finally drew hard, her primal instinct for survival taking over, until her feeding became frenzied. I continued to rub her back. "That's it, Lalka, take what you need."

I was old. She could take far more blood from me before I would feel the effects.

The way I felt in that moment, she could have it all.

The sound of cars, several of them in the distance, reached me. The vampire court had been summoned. We needed to leave. I stood, Mina still in my arms, still attached to my throat. There were doors leading out to a garden, and I kicked them open and carried her out into the night, running for the cover of trees that surrounded the property.

I had to get her home, then I could deal with this. Yes, I could leave this city, I could take Mina away and make a life with her somewhere else, but I didn't think it would come to that.

Not if I had my way.

I sprinted through the trees that lined the long driveway, away from the prime's mansion, concealed from the cars that were headed toward it. I recognized the court members, all grim-faced and pale.

Fear.

I could smell it even through steel and glass.

They should be afraid.

They should be really fucking afraid.

Seventeen

NERO

I LAID Mina on my bed, while Pretender hovered at the door.

"I'm so sorry. I tried to stop them... I failed you... I..."

I turned to my ward, and he trailed off, his gaze dropping to the floor.

He had nothing to apologize for. He'd fought with everything he had. It was there in the bruises still fading and the bones that still hadn't properly knitted themselves back together. "You almost died in your attempts to save Mina. You fought valiantly, Pretender. You don't owe me an apology. I owe you one. I should have seen this coming. I should have stayed."

He flinched. I'd shocked him.

I'd never apologized to him before, and I'd probably never spared my young ward a kind word in his entire time with me. Why would I when I'd been incapable of empathy, of truly seeing him? "You need to rest, to feed and recover. I'll need you strong for what might come next."

He blinked several times, his eyes bright, then he nodded and limped away. Guilt swarmed me immediately. These new emotions were a lot to deal with, near overwhelming. I didn't like knowing I'd hurt him, and I didn't know how to make it right.

I brushed Mina's hair back from her face. Blinded as I'd been, I'd hurt her as well. "You're home now, Lalka. I promise you I will never leave you vulnerable like that again."

She was unconscious, panting, her chest rising and falling fast, her cheeks flushed. My blood was working its way through her system, repairing the damage done. I had no idea how long she'd be like this, how long it would take for her to wake, but I'd be here when she did.

Taking my phone from my pocket, I scrolled to Constantine's number. His female, his mate, now that he'd fully claimed her, had just been through hell.

For the first time, I understood what my brother was feeling.

I knew what he'd suffered and I knew what asking this of him, asking my brothers this, would mean—but I'd do anything to ensure Mina was safe, and for the first time in centuries, they would understand that as well.

Mina

My eyes were scratchy when I opened them, my throat so dry, and when I ran my tongue over my lips I could feel they were cracked. It felt as if I'd been picked up by a giant and squeezed, as if every last ounce of moisture had been wrung from my body. My hand shook as I reached for the glass of water beside the bed, and as soon as my fingertips brushed the cool glass, memories flooded me.

The elders, their fangs buried deep, tearing at my flesh, ravenously draining my blood...the pain—

"Lalka, you're awake."

I jolted. *Nero.* I hadn't even seen him there. He sat by the bed, leaning forward, his fingers around the glass I'd been reaching for. He wore only a pair of dark tracksuit pants. His feet were bare, and his pale, tattooed chest and arms flexed as he moved.

I'd never seen him like this. "You own tracksuit pants?" I rasped past my dry throat.

His lips twitched. "I do."

I realized I wasn't in my room, that I was in his, in his big bed, surrounded by pillows, the covers pulled up around me.

He held the glass to my lips. "Sip, then you need to feed," he said, his voice low, husky in a way I'd never heard it before.

"What happened?" The elders. That dining room.

Nero had come for me.

He'd arrived at the prime's home and...there were screams—blood.

I sucked in a sharp breath. "You killed them. You killed all of them."

His eyes flashed bright. "Yes."

"You can't...they're the elders." My gaze shot to the door. The court would come. They would barge in at any moment and drag us away. "We need to leave. If you stay, they'll execute you. They'll kill you, Nero."

He put down the glass and gently slid the backs of his fingers along my cheek. "Would that make you sad, Mina? If they killed me? If you couldn't see me ever again?"

I stared into his violet eyes. They were different somehow. "Yes, of course," I said without hesitation. Because I would, despite everything.

He studied me, then moved in that controlled way of his, easing back the covers and lifting me from the bed. Then he climbed in, holding me to him, and pulled the quilt back up so it was covering me completely.

"I can sense your hunger. You need to feed," he murmured.

I did. I was so incredibly hungry. Placing my hand on his smooth chest, I pressed my nose to his skin and breathed in his comforting scent. How was it possible that this male, who had been so cold when he first brought me here, could give me that kind of solace, could be a safe place for me. I never thought it was possible. I'd wanted it, but deep down, I didn't believe I could have it, not with him, not really. His arms were around me, his scent so good it had distracted me. I lifted my head. "The court. Nero. We need to leave, we need to—"

"You're safe. We're all safe. I promise. Now feed."

"How...how can we be safe?"

"My brothers and I spoke with the court, they...decided to see things our way. The prime and the other elders broke their own laws when they took you from my home, when they...did what they did to you. And after some coaxing, the court acknowledged that truth and admitted the elders had been taking advantage of their power for some time."

"They didn't know how to stop them?"

He shook his head. "Turns out, I did them a favor."

Relief flooded me. "Thank you," I whispered, and not just for the blood. "If you hadn't come for me—"

"You don't need to thank me, Lalka." His gaze caught and held mine. "I will always come for you, no matter what."

This was a new version of Nero, as if the male he'd buried deep had finally reached the surface. "What happens now? Who will be prime?"

He carefully slid his fingers into my hair and gently held the back of my head. "Enough talking," he said, encouraging me to bite.

I felt warm and safe and cared for. So I nuzzled his tattooed throat, sliding my tongue along the pulsing vein there, taking in more of his reassuring scent, tasting him.

"Mina," he said roughly, impatiently.

I realized I was tormenting us both for some reason. I sucked on his skin gently, and his fingers dug in where they rested on my hip, a low growl rolling from deep in his chest.

I bit down slowly, and he hissed, then cursed.

His cock grew hard beneath me.

"No one will ever hurt you again, my precious Lalka," he said, his deep voice vibrating through me in a way that lifted pleasurable goose bumps all over my skin.

Everything about this moment—the taste of his blood, his arms around me, the proof that he desired me—was perfect. Even after the horror of what happened, I felt content, because I was with Nero. I knew with everything in me that he meant what he said. He would never let anyone hurt me, not ever again.

I fed while Nero murmured low, encouraging me to drink until I was full. I did, drinking until the thirst subsided and I was drowsy and warm. I slid my tongue over the bite I'd made, sealing it, and rested my head against his chest.

"How are you feeling?" he asked.

"Still a little weak, but I can feel my strength coming back, especially now." I pressed my hand to his chest, sliding it higher, my fingers drifting over the spot I'd just fed from. "You said no one will ever hurt me again."

"And I meant it," he said, and I felt a tremor move through him.

"You can't lock me away to do that. Not again, Nero. You have to promise me, you won't ever do that again." I held his gaze. "I'm not Dorotha. You won't lose me as well."

He jolted under me, making it clear what I'd just said had reached him, had gotten through, that I'd been right. Losing his sister had affected him deeply, and still did, even if he hadn't realized it. "I almost did, Lalka. I almost lost you."

"But you saved me. Promise me," I said again.

He nodded, swallowing audibly. "I promise," he said roughly.

"Thank you," I said, keeping my hand on his chest, his cool skin against my palm, needing that contact, that connection with him even though I was literally in his lap.

He stared down at me with a look in his eyes I'd never seen before. That stare wasn't cold, it was anything but.

"Nero?"

He slid the backs of his fingers down the side of my face again, then turned his hand to cup my cheek. "Do you think you could ever truly care for me, Lalka? Do you think..." He swallowed thickly. "Do you think you could love someone like me?"

His question shocked me, but not as much as the longing I now recognized in that unwavering stare. He wanted me to love him. He'd said it, the night of the blood moon ceremony. He'd wanted my love even then, even when he'd been devoid of emotion, even when he wasn't capable of feeling it or returning it himself.

My love.

He'd called me that, hadn't he? When he'd rescued me. His broken voice echoed through my head, the way he'd stared down at me while I'd been strapped to that table. "And do you love me, Nero?"

He blinked down at me. "Do I love you?" He swiped his thumb over the apple of my cheek. "I have this...constant ache in my chest, and the thought of you being hurt fills me with rage, but seeing you hurt, seeing you being hurt—it cracked me wide open. I would destroy anyone who dared lay a finger on you, and I'd enjoy their screams while I did it. I would kill the elders all over again without a moment's thought if I could, but I'd make it slower this time. Your comfort, your happiness, your pleasure and safety, they're all I care about now, Mina." There was another gentle slide of his thumb across my cheek as his gaze brightened. "Do I love you? Yes, I think... No." He shook his head. "No, I'm sure of it, my precious Lalka. I love you. I am in love with you."

I'd never heard him speak like that. How could I doubt it? How could I doubt that look in his eyes? "I love you too." The words slipped from me easily, because I did. It was new and fragile, and it stood on a foundation that others might not believe in. But I believed in it, in what we were building together, I believed in us.

Nero was cold, calculated, terrifying...to everyone but me. For me he burned. For me he would kill. For me he would do anything to make sure I was safe and cared for.

He was everything I didn't know I wanted.

"You truly love me, Lalka?" he rasped.

"Yes," I whispered and reached up to hold the side of his face like he often did mine. His cool skin was no longer a shock, it was perfect, as comforting as his scent. "I want to be your mate, Nero, in truth. Now. Tonight."

He smiled, flashing his fangs, and the beauty of it, of a smile he felt deeply, stole my breath. "I want to make you my mate more than anything, Mina. But taking you slowly, tenderly, in this bed tonight, isn't our way, is it, my precious little doll? When I make you mine in truth for the first time, when I claim you, when I make you my mate, it should be primal and raw. I want that for us, and I think you do too?"

He wanted to chase me, catch me, hold me down. My body heated, my heart instantly picking up speed. I nodded, my throat tight.

"Yes," he said, and he brushed my hair back, so gently, with so much reverence my heart ached. "I thought you'd feel that way, my perfect little Lalka."

I didn't want to wait, I wanted everything he said, now. "When?" I asked, my voice husky with need.

He smiled again. "When you're fully recovered?"

"When will that be?"

He chuckled low, and my stomach fluttered. "After I've fed you several more times and you don't look so pale." As he ran his fingers through my hair, I caught a glimpse of something and grabbed his hand.

There was a gold ring on his finger—old, no, ancient, the top of it was a square with a swirling design stamped into it. My gaze shot up to his. "The court made you prime?"

The muscle in his jaw pulsed. "Yes. My brothers and I are the new elders."

He wouldn't want that. He'd done it for me. "But..."

"All will be well, Mina. There is nothing for you to worry

about except getting better, yes?" Then he kissed me gently and laid my head against his chest. "Now rest. You look exhausted."

I wanted to argue, to ask what this meant for him, for us, but my eyes were heavy and he was right, I'd never been more tired.

~

I woke with my fangs buried in Nero's throat, my skin hot and prickled with sweat and a deep throb that made me whimper. I'd been dreaming of Nero, he'd chased me, he'd—I quivered.

He was stroking my face, and I took his hand in mine and pushed it down between my thighs, spreading them to make room.

He growled, the rough sound making me shiver.

"Tell me what you were dreaming about?" he said in the quiet darkness.

He spread my pussy with his fingers, sliding them through my slickness. "You."

"What was I doing? Tell me," he demanded as he pushed a long, thick finger inside me.

I cried out, fisting his shirt. "You...you were chasing me. You... *Oh gods*," I groaned when he pushed in a second finger, stretching me.

"I was what? Tell me, Mina."

He thrust into me faster, deeper. If it was anyone but him, I'd be too scared to say, to share my deepest darkest desires. "It was dark, I was...scared. There were noises, then you were there, and you...you chased me, you chased me down, and you were wild, uncontrollable...you—" I cried out when he used his thumb against my clit while he continued to thrust inside me. "You threw me down and tore off my clothes... You shoved my legs apart and... and rammed your cock inside me..." As I said it, he snarled and added another finger, filling me ruthlessly.

I screamed, and my inner muscles clamped down on him.

He pressed his forehead to the side of mine. "You want me to hold you down, little doll? You want me to let go of my control and fuck you, claim you like the monster I truly am?"

"Yes," I sobbed, rocking against his fingers, soaking them.

He didn't stop until I collapsed against him, panting and quivering. Then slowly, carefully, he slid his fingers from me and kissed my temple. "You please me so much, Mina. That was so incredibly beautiful."

I clung to his shirt, trying to catch my breath. When I finally had myself under control, Nero tilted my head back and looked into my eyes. "If you truly want that, Lalka, I'll give it to you," he rasped.

"I want it," I said, voice shaking. "Please."

I felt a tremble move through him. "Oh, you'll get it, little doll, you just won't know when."

I shivered again, and he chuckled. "Now go back to sleep. I'm right here if you need to come again."

"I love you," I said, pressing close.

He purred deep in his chest. "I love you more."

Eighteen

MINA

Pretender took my bags, and I followed him down the long hall and out to the car.

"How long will it take to get there?" I asked as he loaded my things into the trunk.

"About an hour."

Nero had been spending several hours each day away with court-related business. Now he was prime, there was a lot he needed to deal with, but he'd promised me a few days away. We were going to one of his homes outside of the city, which sounded lovely. Nero said it was the perfect place for me to rest and recuperate, but I was one hundred percent back to full strength, if only I could make him see that.

He was meeting me at the house tonight, so Pretender had been tasked with taking me, in case his meeting ran late.

I got in the back seat, put my new headphones in, and started the playlist I'd made for the drive. Then I opened the messages and texted Nero that we were leaving the city. He'd bought me a phone a few days ago. I loved it. I loved that I could talk to him whenever I wanted to, even when he was away from the apartment.

His reply came almost instantly.

Nero: *You were looking tired this morning. Drink the blood I left for you and I'll see you later tonight*

I hadn't noticed the insulated cup in the cup holder until now. I took a sip, and my taste buds came alive. The blood was still warm. He thought of everything when it came to my well-being.

How the heck was I going to convince him that I was better? I wanted to be his mate in truth, but that would never happen when he'd convinced himself that I was still sickly and frail.

I leaned back, listening to my music, and drank the blood, while I tried to think of what I could do to help him get past his overprotectiveness. I was stronger than I'd ever been. A constant diet of his blood had ensured that.

Sleeping beside him every night, wrapped in his arms, certainly helped as well.

I was well rested, well fed, and I just wanted to put what happened to me behind us. I wanted to show him I was strong enough to be his mate.

I closed my eyes and must have drifted off, because I woke to Pretender cursing viciously. The car was stopped on a dark, tree-lined road.

I sat up straighter. "What's going on?"

"Fucked if I know. It just stopped." His fingers curled around the steering wheel. "Fuck," he bit out again.

"How far from the house are we?"

He glanced at me in the rearview mirror. "We're on the property now, but it's surrounded by close to a hundred acres of forest-land." He shoved the door open. "I'll go get the car Nero keeps at the house."

"I'm coming with you," I said, because it was creepy out here.

"It'll only take me fifteen minutes if I run. You're not fast enough. Plus I'll have to come back with the car for the bags anyway." He got out.

"Hang on. I'd rather not stay here on my—"

He poked his head in the door. "You have nothing to be afraid of out here, Mina. The sooner I leave, the sooner I'll be back."

"No, but..."

He shut the door and took off before I could finish what I was saying, running so fast, he was a blur, and blending into the shadows moments later. He was right. I couldn't run like that. I was fast, but nothing like him or Nero. Not yet.

The quiet darkness settled around me and nerves instantly swirled in my belly. I pulled out my phone and hit Nero's number.

No reply.

He always answered.

I clutched the phone in my lap, startling when it chimed a moment later.

Nero: *Sorry, still in a meeting. I'll call you as soon as it's over.*

It was breezy outside and the trees swayed in a way that made it look like something was moving around out there. I studied the shadows. *It's just the trees, there's nothing there.*

Still, the antsy, nervous feeling grew.

Pretender would be back soon. He was fast. It wouldn't take him long—

A sound, high-pitched and grating, filled the car. It was like—I spun around—something was scratching against the outside of it. A tree branch? No, I wasn't close enough to any trees. I spun back when I caught something out of the corner of my eye, something dark. *You're seeing things.* I quickly locked the doors.

Oh gods. I spun the other way. I saw it again, something dark rushed past, but this time it hit the car, making it jolt.

I shrieked.

My phone rang and I nearly jumped out of my skin. Nero's name flashed in the darkness. I shoved myself low and quickly answered. "Nero, I'm scared. I—"

"Give me your word, Mina."

I froze. "My word?"

He didn't reply, just waited.

It was happening. Oh gods, it was finally happening. The car hadn't broken down, Nero had planned it. "Pink," I whispered for some reason.

"You have five seconds to get out of the car and run for the trees."

My heart slammed into my throat. Nero was out there. "Or what?" I said, my voice shaking from the way my heart pounded.

"Or I will tear off the door and drag you into the forest myself." He slammed into the car again, and I barely held in another shriek.

"Nero—"

"Five, four—"

"What are you going to do?"

"Make you scream," he said. "Then moan."

My pussy contracted as my fear shot higher.

"Three."

I shoved the door open.

"Two," he said.

"Oh gods," I gasped and burst from the car, sprinting into the trees.

"One." He laughed darkly. "Run, little doll."

I knew it was Nero, and I knew he'd never hurt me, but my adrenal glands did not. Everything in me roared that I needed to run for my life.

A snarl came from somewhere behind me but still a little distance away. Thankfully, Nero had taken me shopping a couple of days ago. I was wearing yoga pants, a sweatshirt, and jogging shoes, so I didn't feel the branches slapping at my body or the rough forest floor beneath my feet. Another sound came from behind me, to the right this time. The fear spiked with excitement, and I dug my heels in and sprinted harder, faster than I ever had in my life.

The blood pumping through my veins was hot and rich, and my lungs were full of the damp, earthy scents of the forest.

A *whoop* came next, closer this time and on the left.

He was closing in, toying with me.

My body's response to being chased flooded my nervous system. I was dizzy, felt out of control, my pulse racing, my mind spinning, my heart thudding wildly. It was primal, and there was this knot of desire low in my belly, unfurling, spreading out, stealing my breath.

He tugged at my sweatshirt as he flashed past.

A low, dark laugh echoed to my left. I spun around—

He tugged my hair as he blurred past again, and my hair unraveled from the knot at the back, falling around my shoulders.

My lungs burned, the panic growing wider as my panties grew wetter.

I stumbled and caught myself, but my next few steps were unsteady, my gait thrown off. I stepped on the root of a tree the wrong way and fell. Scrambling, I tried to get up—

Nero pounced, knocking me to the ground. I screamed, my adrenaline forcing me to switch from flight to fight mode. I clawed at the earth beneath me as he tore at my clothes, shoving up my sweatshirt, then using it to secure my wrists.

"No," I shouted, fighting hard. "Stop."

"I can smell your cunt, and it definitely doesn't want me to stop." He flipped me to my back, wrenching my tights down my legs. My bare ass should have been on the damp earth, but there was something soft beneath me, something warm.

Pinning my bound hands over my head with one hand, he shoved up my shirt with the other and tugged down my bra, exposing my breasts to the cool, damp air.

Leaning in, he sunk his teeth into the side of my breast, drawing hard. I cried out and bucked, gasping for breath, fighting as my pussy clamped down hard. He lifted his head and flashed his bloody teeth and fangs as he let my blood fall from his lips, dripping it onto my nipples and down my stomach. "Scream," he growled.

I did, I screamed and thrashed, panting, as he licked and sucked every bit of blood from my breasts and stomach, still holding me immobile, pinned beneath him.

When he finally lifted his head again, I was heaving for my next breath, feeling weak and desperate for him, to feel him inside me—for him to make me his.

Still pinning my wrists over my head with one hand, he undid his belt with the other. "You came out here looking to get claimed by a monster, didn't you, little doll?"

I shook my head, kicking and bucking, and with each wild and failed attempt to get free, I got hotter, slicker. "No. Get off me. Stop. *Stop!*"

The head of his cock brushed my pussy, and I bucked harder.

Nero's nostrils flared. "Fuck," he groaned. "Liar. You're dripping. So fucking desperate for your twisted male to stuff you full."

I snapped my fangs at him, and he laughed.

"You are mine, Lalka, and after this, you'll be mine for eternity." He pinned me with a dark stare as he took something from his pocket. Pink diamonds glittered in the dim light.

The choker he'd gifted me for our blood moon ceremony. He secured it around my throat, leaving his hand there, and squeezed lightly. "Mine."

The heavy weight around my throat was like another claiming. I loved it.

He was giving me everything I'd asked for, everything I needed. This was perfect. He was perfect. "Then do it," I bit out, panting hard, wanting this so bad I trembled. "Do it!"

He slammed his hips forward, filling me completely with one hard thrust. I threw my head back, an animalistic sound bursting from me as I came instantly around him.

Nero roared, thrusting into me with vampire speed. It was too much, he was too big, this feeling was too wild, still I arched my back, lifting my hips so I could take more, so I could welcome more of this out-of-control feeling and give every part of my mind, body, and soul to Nero, to my mate. I came and came until I was slick with sweat and shaking uncontrollably.

"Look what you do to me," he snarled, slowing his thrusts, now slamming into me hard and deep. "Only you make me feel this way, only you can draw out the monster inside me."

"Prove it, bite me," I moaned helplessly. "Make me yours."

He didn't hesitate. He turned my head to the side, and sank his fangs deep into my throat. I came again, a raw sound that I'd never made in my life unleashing from deep within me. He drew hard, and my pussy contracted with each deep pull. I shuddered and moaned and clawed at his back.

Nero sealed his bite, then rolled so we were facing each other, and led my mouth to his throat. I knew what I had to do, and I struck, biting him as deeply as he had me, sucking hard on his vein. His cock pulsed inside me, as he gripped my ass, holding me to him, and stayed there, filling me, coming for me.

He continued to thrust until we were both utterly spent. I lazily dragged my tongue over his skin, sealing my bite, and Nero rolled me to my back again, looking down at me.

"My perfect little Lalka." He brushed my hair back gently, in that reverent way that still managed to surprise me. "My precious mate. I will love you, Mina, protect and cherish you, until the end of existence."

I slid my hand over his shoulder. "And I will love you right back, my beautiful, vicious mate. You are mine, and you are all I will ever need..." I slid my hand lower, over his chest, and froze.

Nero went on instant alert, searching the trees, then frowned and looked back down. "What is it?"

"Your heart." I blinked rapidly. "Nero...can't you feel it? Your heart's beating."

He stilled.

Taking his hand, I lifted it to his chest. "Do you feel it now?"

His throat worked, his Adam's apple sliding up and down. "I feel it," he rasped and pressed his forehead to mine. "I feel it," he said again and swallowed thickly. "It's beating for you, my love. Just for you."

Epilogue

NERO

Seven months later

I SIPPED my drink and closed my laptop.

"You need anything else?" Pretender asked.

It was late, both clubs were closed and I'd finished working for the night. "No. Get some rest, tomorrow will be busy." He nodded and headed for the door. "Are you seeing anyone?" I asked before he could leave, the words slipping from me out of nowhere. Though I had been wondering, now that I had Mina.

Pretender paused at the door. My interest in his life still surprised him, and on occasion surprised me as well. I held...great affection for him. Mina had unlocked my emotions and, seven months later, I was still adjusting to it. No one saw me this way except my mate and, on occasion, Pretender, and, of course, my brothers. I loved my Lalka with my entire heart. What I felt for my ward, for my brothers was, I guess, a kind of love as well.

In other words, this was still confusing as fuck.

Pretender shrugged. "I don't have time for friends or lovers."

There was a strange look in his eyes. "You're young, you should make time for enjoyments."

He grinned, but his smile didn't reach his eyes, something I never would have noticed before Mina changed me. "You know why I can't do that," he said roughly. "Someone always ends up getting hurt."

I realized in that moment, that the someone was probably him. "One day you will find your mate, and—"

"No disrespect, Nero, but not everyone is destined for what you have. We don't all have someone like Mina waiting for us to find them." He shook his head. "I'm happy as I am."

He was lying about the way he felt, something else I might have missed before. I studied him, his face that could have been carved by the angels themselves—beauty like that, it came at a price, which was why he covered his face most of the time. I'd named him Pretender when his parents first left him here because he'd imitated me constantly. I'd asked him if he wanted to rule my kingdom, if he wanted to be a warrior and run my clubs one day, and he'd said yes immediately. I couldn't even remember what his birth name was. "You needed more from me over the years, and I was too blind to see it. You should know that I consider you family…and should you ever need anything, anything at all, ask and it's yours."

He nodded, then cleared his throat. "Thank you. Good night, Nero."

He strode away and I sat back in my chair. Living a cold and emotionless life had blinded me to so very much, and I was still relearning to read those around me.

There was a soft knock at the door and my mate walked in. As soon as I saw her, I warmed. It started in the center of my chest and radiated out. Only Mina did that to me, only she warmed me to the bone and made me feel vulnerable, almost human.

She crossed my office and I slid my chair back so she could climb into my lap. "I was missing you," she said.

"I was missing you too."

Her head tilted to the side. "I saw Pretender on my way up, is he okay?"

I ran the backs of my fingers down her cheek, her jaw, to her slender throat. I constantly craved the touch of her skin, her warmth against mine, and there was no resisting it. I didn't even try anymore. As always, she wore the velvet choker I'd gotten her after we mated. It was lighter than the one she wore to our blood moon ceremony, more suitable for everyday wear and had a small pink diamond that sat at the base of her neck. She said it made her feel closer to me, as if my hands were always on her even when we were apart. I loved that, more than I could express, because seeing her wear it, knowing she wore it when I wasn't with her made me feel the same way.

"He says not, but I think that perhaps he's lonely. Staying loyal to someone like me, for so long, he's missed out on a lot..." I held her stunning lavender eyes. "I didn't deserve his loyalty. I'm not sure how to repay him for it."

Her smile softened. "You're his father, maybe not by blood but in his heart. He loves you. That's all he wants from you. To know you care about him as well."

"That's easier said than done, Lalka." I realized then that her heart was beating faster than usual. "Is everything all right?"

"Yes." She licked her lips and took my hand. "And, in the meantime, while you're still learning to express your emotions for anyone who isn't me..." She placed my hand on her stomach. "Together, the three of us will make sure Pretender feels part of our family."

"Three?"

She curled her fingers around the side of my throat. "Listen."

I frowned.

"Listen, Nero."

I did. I honed in on the sound of the blood rushing through her veins, the faster-than-usual beat of her heart, the— My eyes shot up to hers as another heartbeat reached me, this one more distant, faster. "A baby," I rasped. "You're having a baby."

Her cheeks were pink, her eyes glistening and bright with happiness as she nodded. "Yes, *we're* having a baby."

I'd noticed subtle changes to her body, but my mate being pregnant with my child had never occurred to me. Her joy made my already stunning bride even more beautiful. I wanted to feel what she did, but instead, fear filled me.

Mina never missed anything when it came to me. "You're not happy?"

"I'm terrified," I said, telling her the truth. "What if I... What if I hurt them the same way I did Pretender, and you? What if...what if I've reached my capacity to love and I don't have any more to give? The way I love you, Lalka, you take up my entire heart."

She didn't look at me like a monster. No, her smile returned, and she covered my hand still on her stomach with both of hers. "There is no capacity. Love is endless, boundless. Listen to that tiny heartbeat. It's part of you, of us. Our love created the baby growing inside me. You already love them, Nero. You already love our baby."

Gods, I felt it. I felt that small heartbeat inside mine. I was still terrified, but she was right, Mina was always right. A fierceness filled me like nothing before. "I'll kill anyone who tries to harm them, Lalka."

"Oh, I know you will, and so will I," she said as she shifted, straddling me instead. Her fingers worked my belt, undoing my trousers and releasing my instantly hardening cock. Positioning me, she sat, and I filled her with a groan.

Her arms wrapped around my neck as she rode me slowly, making love to her mate.

I was a different male because of her, for her, a better one, and I would do whatever it took to stay that way for my precious Lalka and our child.

"I love you, Nero." She gasped as she moved on top of me, her little fangs sliding down, preparing to strike.

I held her tight to me. "I love you more."

Also by Sherilee Gray

Rocktown Ink:

Beg For You

Sin For You

Meant For you

Bad For You

All For You

Just for You

The Smith Brothers:

Mountain Man

Wild Man

Solitary Man

Lawless Kings:

Shattered King

Broken Rebel

Beautiful Killer

Ruthless Protector

Glorious Sinner

Merciless King

Boosted Hearts:

Swerve

Spin

Slide

Spark

Axle Alley Vipers:

Crashed

Revved

Wrecked

Black Hills Pack:

Lone Wolf's Captive

A Wolf's Deception

Stand Alone Novels:

Breaking Him

While You Sleep

About the Author

Sherilee Gray is a kiwi girl and lives in beautiful New Zealand with her husband and their two children. When she isn't writing sexy contemporary or paranormal romance, searching for her next alpha hero on Pinterest, or fueling her voracious book addiction, she can be found dreaming of far off places with a mug of tea in one hand and a bar of chocolate in the other.

To find out about new releases, giveaways, events and other cool stuff, sign up for my newsletter!

www.sherileegray.com